5 SWEET HOLIDAY STORIES

5 SWEET HOLIDAY STORIES

SOFT AND TENDER TALES, SORELY NEEDED

MICHÈLE LAFRAMBOISE

 ECHOFICTIONS

Cover Design by Echofictions

Cover pic © Deposit photos

Cover author photo © Frédéric Gagnon

Inside author photo © Gilles Gagnon

Inside illustrations © Michèle Laframboise

Published by

 ECHOFICTIONS

Mississauga, ON

ISBN 978-1-990824- 24-1 ebook

ISBN 978-1-990824-23-4 Paperback

INTRODUCTION

In difficult times, when a cold darkness spreads over the countries and oppression threatens the most vulnerable amoung us, a pick-me up story can be the best resistance tool for weary souls. Those tales of love and courage will lift the veil of sadness and pump up enough joy to rise and fight another day!

In those *5 Sweet Holiday Stories*, follow hard-working, lonely women confronting adversity or coming to a fork in the road where the delicate balance of their orderly life hang. Five women, each meeting her own challenge, will discover a special magic that opens the hearts. You will even meet a character from the previous collection!

An inn keeper struggling to keep her parents' dream alive will find a new hope. A daring escape by a ballet dancer sets the table for a tender reunion, years later. A radio voice beckons a depressed musician on to better times. A divorced mother, worried about the adult daughter she left in New York, settles for a simple good time alone in beautiful Hawaii, not expecting any complication.

And a young stuntwoman stuck in a toxic relationship gets an uncanny visit on Christmas Eve, and a wish of the heart she didn't know she craved will be granted by the best Authority in the matter!

May your winter days be filled with light and hope!

5 SWEET HOLIDAY STORIES

In honor of Jo Beverley,
mistress of romances!

THE DEER MOUNTAIN CANNON

BETH SANDERLING PUT one bare hand over the glass of the Rosemary Inn's front window, the other stabilizing the fragrant branches of the decorated pine. Her print vanished like a ghost as soon as she released the pressure. She had barely felt the cold that should reign supreme at this time, a December more akin to a moody November.

She stepped out, past the veranda with winter-resistant chairs and cupholders, and descended the stairs to avenge the last sun rays of the short day. Outside the Inn, a frozen lawn of dead yellow grass fell in a gentle slope to the entrance gate (a grand name for a wooden frame standing all by itself by the main regional road, looking as lonely as she felt.)

How she yearned for a white, smooth blanket!

The pair of mature maple trees flanking the pathway to her door had shed their riotous colors weeks ago, but no snow had materialized since, except shy flurries quickly dispatched by the mild temperatures.

Which was not the problem of the neighboring ski resort, she thought, gloomily.

The mountain face was shaved into serpentine trails, crowned by a peaked resort house covered with so many lights it seemed like a Christmas tree had landed on the top. Specks of bright fabric danced gracefully down the serpentine slopes –a few less gracefully--, their skis lifting powdery clouds in their wake.

She remembered what Deer Mountain had been, when her parents had built the Inn, a beautiful escape with hiking trails and a spectacular view from the top, a reward for the efforts spent on the way. (And yes, Beth had actually seen the shy deer.)

Then the mountain had been bought, the zoning changed somehow (*not somehow*, her mother had said, some-*money*.) Money had changed pockets, and the mountain had been hacked and shaved to accommodate the ultraposh resort. The admission fee cost a small fortune.

As for the deer, the herd had fled, and none had since been seen in the patch of mature tree forest at the back of the inn, where guests could walk on snowshoes or country-ski on winter.

But at that time, Beth had been a jolly student dead set on her own pursuit of happiness. It had taken two broken relationships and her failing at getting a decent job to teach her the ways of the world. Now she could only lament what had been, hoping the herd of deers lived happy somewhere else.

The western "ultra-expert" slope ran down like a white tongue to lick her property line (and still so strange to think of her property, now). She could get a better view of the skiers, all clad in exotic, extraterrestrial fabrics, their heads swiveling to take in the cozy little Inn her parents had built.

As Beth stood there in her rapidly cooling sweater--a bit envious of the skiers if she was honest with herself--, one lean silhouette veered in a tight turn, splashing snow in a wide arc.

The skier slowed down to complete the turn, powerful legs cemented together, knees absorbing the multiple shocks of the surface. Suddenly, he (she?) waved at her, one gloved hand raising the pole, its tip tracing another arc in the air, the bulbous goggles flashing a last orange ray her way.

She blinked, because the smile under those insectoid goggles had felt as luminous as the last sun rays.

Good dentist, she thought, waving back to the stranger. Not her habit, but hey, it felt nice to be acknowledged.

She followed with her eyes the receding violet-blue back, legs and poles now pushing hard downslope, until the skier was engulfed in the crowd surrounding the monstruous lift machine.

Of course, they were all loaded like gold bricks, residing in the town's posh hotels, or at this pricey, peaky resort.

Her left knee throbbed as she stepped closer to the slope. It has never healed perfectly after her dramatic fall in the Olympic qualifications' trials. Restoring her kneecap to full coordination would have required a very costly operation that her insurance provider had rejected.

Beth had tried the slopes after, but her legs had become separate entities, left divorced from right.

She thought of the skier, those knees, so perfectly matched. She couldn't guess his or her age, but if the person was young enough, a sports career was an option.

But, no, would a seventeen-year-old acknowledge some thirty-ish woman in a loose pullover and faded jeans?

At that moment, a white plume shot up from the mountain flank, a geyser of synthetic crystals arcing to fall on the ski corridors.

The cannon spewing the artificial snow was so large a guardrail surrounded it, like those pieces in the war movies. And almost as noisy, with the mix of air and water forced into a hasty marriage. She had expected a person manning it, but the circular platform around the cylinder was empty. Had they automatized the process? Of course, the investors had deep pockets to impose winter on the landscape!

She noticed how a bunch of snow had been pushed over the edge of the trail, spilling over the Inn's property. Well, she thought, at least she could make a decent snowman out of that crest. And mayyybe it would draw some curious to her holly-decorated door.

Beth gazed at the frothy plume, dejected. Who was she

to entertain such ridiculous notions? Should she have splurged for a cannon instead of waiting for Mister Frost?

The attraction power of the **ski** resort was like a black hole to her tiny, tiny star.

A star that could, very soon, be engulfed in this vast money well.

IN THE PAST YEARS, the resort's owners had tried to buy the Inn that sat so close to their slopes (to tear it down and build a swanky spa). Beth's mother had rejected all offers. Maybe her father would have relented, but he had suffered a fatal heart attack ten years ago.

Beth's fingers dug into the knitted sweater, its elaborate red, white and violet swirls a testimony to her mother's talent. How she missed her! Rosemary's strong, assertive spirits had endured invasive treatments of the cancer for two years, but the rogue bunch of egoist cells had prevailed.

The last five months of her mom's illness, Beth had managed the Inn by herself with a few faithful hands, rejecting the buying offers.

As Christmas approached, she had let go of the cook, for his own family vacations. However, he had left a bunch of hearty soups in the fridge, along with an assortment of fresh meat pies (along with the veggie option), all easy to reheat for a dinner guest. For the Inn's breakfast, Beth had confidence in her own prowess with the crepe pan, turning eggs and omelets.

She walked up the slope leading to her home, her bad knee throbbing. Inside, she was greeted by the rich aromas of good food baking. She was a decent cook, at least for desserts. She had made a lot, as if the pastries would conjure more guests. Chocolate chips cookies were sitting in the oven, waiting to be appreciated. She thought of the blue skier, wishing for company at least, if not a rooming guest.

Beth could not help seeing her mother's fairy touch in this warm and welcoming space: the original Rosemary, her magical fingers conjuring into existence fantastic scarfs, mittens, sweaters that the other schoolchildren envied Elisabeth.

Even long after Beth and her brothers had grown into moody teens, then harried adults and (for her brothers) worried parents, Rosemary found time to make countless sweaters, the intricate swirls being her trademark, all while managing the Inn she and her husband had built.

And that management now leaned heavily on Beth's thin shoulders. She had inherited the place, with the worries that went with it.

Like the absence of snow.

Like the absence of guests.

Like, oh, the jolly financial statements coming up for the next fiscal year! She tried not to think of the pile of invoices on her desk waiting to be sated.

And, speaking of invoices, she had almost stepped on a yellow envelope lying by the front door, probably slipped through the mail slot because today was a holiday. No stamps, marked with a too-familiar triangular logo.

Oh, not again! Her mother was not six months in her grave, and that horrid promoter kept pestering her with offers, week after week! She picked up the envelope.

But the format was different, not a long business envelope this time. More like a greeting card. Not wanting to waste her time, she ripped it open.

Yup, a smiling Santa, with the words *Have yourself a nice Christmas*, in scarlet letters, no signature. Like those impersonal, industrial low-grade cards her last employer had sent, two months before firing her.

She ground her teeth, a habit her mom had stamped off.

Not a team player, the company's HR clean-cut man had said. Well, Beth certainly hadn't wanted to play her supervisor's games, after hours.

Your values do not align with ours. That had been for questioning their delocalization of hardware plants to some Asian subcontractor. And it was maybe linked to said supervisor calling her a lesbian after she rejected his advances.

Then she felt an icy cold fear trickling over her spine.

Over the word *nice*, someone had scrawled "last" in a tone of red ink to match the inscription.

A threat?

Beth recalled all those one-star Internet reviews piling one over the other in the late summer, an impossible number for a place with only three (very neat and clean) guest rooms. *Small is beautiful*, her mom had said. Never before had those three rooms been empty.

Beth longed for her tiny apartment in Chicago, but the sky-rocketing rents had cemented her resolve to come here. She had revelled in the Appalachian landscape in full glory, and the happy travelers' happiness after a day's hike. Then, not long after the first envelope landed with an offer, the flow of visitors had dwindled to a few drops, and the ski resort mountain loomed larger than ever.

Her fingers were leaving spots on the crisp cardboard. She took slow breath after slow breath to keep her dark emotions at bay. Beth smelled something burning in the small restaurant kitchen, the cake and biscuits, with... was it a hint of seared chocolate?

Cursing her distraction, she flung the card and spun on her flat running shoes to check the state of the kitchen nation. The pot of bubbling fudge was bleeding chocolate over the range; the cookies in the oven were turning a too-dark shade of brown.

She donned the mitts and rescued cookies from the inferno and poured as much of the fudge into another pot. She would have been proud to serve the guests, but none had materialized yet.

Her mother had fairy fingers on the pans and pots and her gingerbread cookies had just the right among of ginger.

Now Beth had to work double, eying the empty tables at the dining room.

Outside, darkness had fallen. A garland of lampposts turned the ski slopes into vanilla tears, inhabited by the moving specks.

This would be a good hour for guests to come in. No advanced reservations had been made, but she would be perfectly content to greet stray tourists.

She went back to her own room in the basement to refresh herself and change into a pair of midnight blue pants, choosing with it her favorite pullover, angel-blue with knitted white flurries.

Like a silent prayer to call up the snow.

BETH'S WISH had still not been granted an hour later, as she tidied the kitchen for, sigh, another empty, guest-less night. She wasn't in a mood to wash the dishes and let the plates and scrubbed trays stew in the soapy water.

A double *bang* echoed, muffled by the house, followed by a velvety *floof*.

Fireworks, already? The promoters really wanted to impress their guests! But wasn't it too soon? Then her weary eyes caught the orange glow that silhouetted her Christmas tree.

Beth rushed to the front window, all sluggishness

chased away by the spectacle. The bases of both maples were engulfed in flames.

Her mom-and-pop maples.

The threat bounced in her skull as she grabbed a pan. Then she ran outside, hoping against all reason to catch the perps red-handed.

Beth, pint-sized, without any training, holding an emptied fudge pan, shot between the flaming trees, through the framed entrance, lungs and feet pumping, bad knee forgotten.

The cold air clogged her throat as she huffed, already out of breath (when she had been, so long ago an up-and-coming athlete.) She reached the regional road just in time to see a pair of taillights speeding away, the car melting into the traffic that came and went from the mountain.

Of course she hadn't had time to read the license number.

Now, a host of small fiery tongues was licking the coarse bark of the maples. She smelled the velvety murmur of a fuel fire. The vandals had spread accelerant over the base of the trees. They may have spread some higher because a few flames threatened the lower branches.

She pivoted on the dry grass and ran inside, almost slipped over the horrid card, and freed the foot-long red ABC cylinder from its space under the main counter. The fuel fire was a B type, which her dry chemical extinguisher should kill.

She hoped so.

She pulled the lever, like she had seen on the internet tutorial. The top lever would not budge, what had she forgotten? She felt out of her depth. The bark crackled, the bubbling sap under it hissing angrily.

Fact was, Beth had never used the extinguisher, and neither had her mother, a testament to the cook's ease of managing cooking oil.

Her maple would burn. She eyes the pan, left in the snow. Grabbed it.

Ignoring the frenzied or excited cries of the skiers who had spotted the burning trees, she ran toward the thick crest of snow lining the trail. The war-sized cannon was now silent, but it had spread enough snow to form a white buff at the edge.

She used the same pan to sweep the icy crystals, then ran back to the trees, and cast it over the murmuring flames. Melted water was not the best to douse the flames, but it coated the bark for a few precious seconds. How long would that fuel burn?

Beth pulled her phone from her pant's pocket to call the fire department. She incinerated the thought, her fingers frozen over the dials.

The firefighter truck would take a half-hour to get there, and they would only find the trees turned into a crisp with dead burnt grass all around. Plus, her pair of maples stood a safe distance from the big house, no menace. While so many murderous electrical fires happened during the Holidays…

A frantic run to the edge, a dip of the pan (still smelling of burnt chocolate), rinse and repeat.

She was dipping her pan at the flames, face turned away from the heat, when she glimpsed one skier veering toward her. She barely had time to notice the blue outfit as the silhouette jumped over the property line, taking advantage of the momentum and the piled snow, landing in a puff of powdery snow on the dry grass. The stranger then shook one, then the other ski off, letting go of the poles.

"Step back, step back from the fire!"

Beth's cold ears caught the voice, a *he*, then the urgent tone, before a gloved hand grabbed a shoulder through the thin, clean pullover, and pulled.

She fell backward against a hard nylon cliff, the unwanted contact spurring her to twist, facing the stranger. She had to look up, and up, the ski boots adding inches to his height.

The insectoid goggles had been pushed back over his cap. She noticed then, in the light of the flames, a pair of concerned eyes almost the color of the indigo sky.

Eyes becoming hard as they focused on the fallen red cylinder.

"Get the extinguisher!"

Her brain was not in place.

"I can't open it," she said.

He seized the cylinder.

"Oh, it's the tape."

She had expected a reproach of her silliness, like her last

boyfriend had, so often. But his voice had no negative inflexion as he pulled the transparent sealing tape holding the lever.

The tiny extinguisher released a powerful jet of dry powder, but the skier held it in firm hands as he directed the muzzle toward the closest tree base.

The pale jet covered the flames in a low whisper. It took all of five seconds to save the first, then he moved to the second maple.

Once the flames were doused, the stranger let go of the cylinder.

"You'll have to change it. It's empty."

A fountain of *thank-yous* rose through her mind. But the words caught her throat at the blacked limbs.

"My, dad planted those trees."

He circled the base, tapping the bark. Then, he turned, a reassuring smile showing his even teeth. His brows were united in a curious expression, and the wisps of hair escaping from his cap were dark.

"Your trees may lose a few lower limbs, but they'll survive. Maples are sturdy beasts."

A puff of warmth suffused her, so relieved she felt as her parents' trees.

A shiver ran through her spine, now that the flames were off. Temperatures had fallen close to the freezing point, but the starry sky showed no promise of snow. At last, she managed a weak "thank you," her voice strangled, her emotion tangled.

He picked up the pan. Surprisingly he bent over and drew a long, deep breath. Then, those expressive eyes found her again.

"Er... what were you doing, in this?"

The question, as well as those blue wells, swept her away from her current worries.

"F-fudge," she said. "But it went wrong."

He gave her back the pan, then turned to retrieve his poles and skis.

In that instant, as his heavy ski boots crushed the frozen blades of grass, Beth felt as if the few stars inhabiting the sky were winking off, and she would pass the rest of the night, no, of her *life*, alone. She couldn't believe she was thinking that, but the impression of the abyss gaping at her if he passed the boundary of the resort, -- as in some fairy tales— crushed her lungs into a mass of need.

"I, I have hot chocolate!" she said, her voice stumbling.

The skier paused.

It was the least she could do to reward his timely help. As she turned to the house, her left knee decided to make itself known. She winced as she shifted her weight on her right leg. She would pay for this hasty run.

"Are you well?" he asked.

That voice, showing concern. How long had it been since she heard something similar?

"Knee, acting up," she said, putting up what she hoped was a brave smile.

Her smile winked out when the pain flared up. That decided him.

She didn't protest when his right arm wound under her left.

~

HER FUMBLING WITH THE CUPS, and the hot milk, went unobserved by her guest.

Between the first and the third front step of the inn, names had been exchanged.

Once Beth had reassured him about her knee, he had pulled off his heavy ski boots, the release of the clasps sending loud, dry *ticks*. She remembered those boots from her own sportive days. He was lucky to enjoy skiing. He asked to use the bathroom and went to it, in stockings. Beth surmised he had wanted to dry his own feet.

She learned that Michael had dined early, to avoid the crowds at the posh resort restaurant. Beth had taken out the green porcelain cups of her grandmother and brought the fuming chocolate to the twin armchairs facing the window, her knee relishing the warmth.

Of course, he had wanted to know about the accident that brought her current condition. She told him the Cliff's Notes, not wanting to go into details about the horrendous lack of support by the insurance providers.

Later, as she sipped her hot chocolate (had she gotten

the spice mix right?) looking at the mountain, another plume went up.

"If only it was real snow," she said.

He blew over the surface of his mug, sending a cloud of vapor that framed his eyes.

"Oh, but it is technically snow," he said.

She shook her head, dark hair falling askew.

"Oh, yes of course I know how it is made. But still, it's not the same as snowflakes falling from the sky."

The plume stopped. At this hour, the resort was emptying, but the die-hard skiers had the slopes to themselves. She could see how Michael's clear eyes followed each lone speck.

He must be itching to go back, she thought, dejected.

"Do they need to use the cannons so often?"

Micheal sipped, his tousled hair shining with sweat. She stole a glance at his face, unmarked, except for the crow's line around the eyes that suggested a sense of humor. She didn't need to look at his waist to guess at his good stamina. He was around her own age, but in way much better shape.

"Not often," he said. "But in the night, yes, because the colder temperatures allow snow to build up."

In her training athlete days, she hadn't cared much about the logistics. Also, she had trained in the Rockies, where there was no lack of real snow. Before the accident...

She sipped. Her chocolate had gone lukewarm.

"How come you know so much?" she asked.

"Because it's my job to know about those things."

"What do you do for a living?"

"I work for an insurance company."

Beth felt suddenly cold. The operation, rejected by the insurance. Her grip threatened to break the porcelain mug's handle. Her face must have betrayed her misgivings. He looked at her, puzzled.

"What, what sort of insurance company?" she asked, in a deadpan voice.

If it was a medical insurance company, she would throw the loot out.

Oh, the waste, another part of her thought.

"I inspect places for breaches of safety conditions. Like this resort."

A small *Oh* fluttered off her lips like a baby bird.

"So, not a medical company."

He drained his cup.

"No. And I should have guessed that your knee wasn't treated properly."

She shook her head, her eyes brimming with tears. He let out a short sight.

"When did your accident happen? You told me you were training for the Olympic Games, did you?"

She nodded. She could go on forever, listening to his kind, gravelly voice.

"Listen, Beth, I'm sorry that you had to live through this. You're not the only one falling prey to greed."

He pointed at the blinking resort through the window.

"This place... My father started a ski resort when I was a baby. South of here. I grew up using snow cannons and lift rotors. But I went abroad to study, and once I got back, I learned that my dad' partner had sold the resort to a hedge fund company."

"And is it still active?"

He shook his head, the hair bouncing.

"The hedge fund sold everything: the lift, the snow cannons, the restaurant house... piecemeal, to its own subsidiary that rented it back to what was left of my dad's resort. They also replaced the experienced workers with students. Eventually, the public moved elsewhere. Then, the subsidiary company closed my dad's resort and sold everything for scrap."

"I guess the quality of service had dropped."

"But the shareholders were happy. That's what counted."

"I... know the kind," she said.

His indignation reached a sympathetic fiber inside her. Or, maybe, it was the proximity of this body, the faint smell of sweat from exercise. The thin jersey he had been wearing under his ski vest was hugging the hills and valleys of bulging muscles. She itched to touch the fabric.

She should not tell a stranger of her troubles. But who else?

"That ski resort, out there, wants to buy the Rosemary Inn. To put up a luxury spa in its place."

Her arm, swept to encompass the proud little Inn, and

its two burnt maples. She thought of the card, still lying crumpled on the floor.

"I don't know what to do," she said, letting her tears fall.

Two warm hands took hers.

"Beth, I am so sorry! I should have known: such a quint nice little house, with the forest back there."

His face, so close, sent her heart in a flurry of beats.

"There were deers here," she said, hiccupping. "They disappeared."

Her tears escaped, containment breach in her eyes, as if she was turning into liquid. And there, like a wave his arms encircled her, and her sobbing head rested against his own strong beating heart. The jersey was a kind of synthetic fiber, soft.

It was a strange contradiction how she could feel both sad and contented at the same time. His comforting hands stroked her hair sending tiny electric charges in her brain.

When she had shed a liter of tears (by her own estimate) and the sadness receded behind a fuzzy peace, he took his hands away.

"Can you show me that greeting card?"

AFTER HE EXAMINED THE CARD, he had, with her trailing after, inspected all the doors and windows, pointing out weaknesses. Michael was a good insurance worker. He moved a lot, going where his bosses asked, to detect improprieties.

"The Deer Mountain Resort is a client of my company, but they had filed many claims that didn't add up. And I know, by skiing there, that the personnel are made of illegal immigrants."

"Unqualified, and dependant," she said.

She pushed the rear door's deadbolt.

"I guess the poor joes who lit up your trees were under orders. If caught, they would have been on their own."

Her indignation peaked. Not only they threatened her, but they exploited powerless people to do their deed!

"I don't know how to fight them," she said. "They are crushing my business."

He turned from the tree he had been admiring.

"Speaking of business," he said. "I would very much like to rent a room in this nice place. Do you think you could accommodate me?"

A PART OF THE NIGHT, Beth was acutely aware of every noise her new guest made in the upper room. The steps, the water faucet, the shower (and there, her febrile imagination did a number on her) and the mattress' springs. At a point, she heard his level voice, talking on the phone.

She listened, capturing each noise in a coffer so she would remember it for a long time. Such a good person was not for her. And besides, he would be gone back to his own place, or to another inspection assignment, soon.

She felt grown up and reasonable.

So why was she miserable, tossing in her bed near the office?

THE NEXT DAY was Christmas Eve. Clear skies and cold.

As for the snow... no show.

Beth's spirit sank. She did her best to hide her disappointment as she played the hostess, slapping up a hearty breakfast with egg omelet and pancakes. He must have noticed her expression, because when she put down the pancake plate, he touched her forearm, gently.

"Please, eat with me," he said.

And she did, bringing new pancakes with the costly maple syrup. The taste melted in her mouth as she ate, in a peaceful silence.

She cast several glances out the window, to her sad, yellow grassy lawn.

"The forecast says no snow," she said.

He paused, a tasty morsel halfway to his sensual mouth.

"Snow on Christmas, you know, is overrated."

His manners had reverted to politeness, as if last night's comforting embrace had never occurred.

"I know," she said. "It's all our pollution coming around, messing with the climate and winter."

They made small talk over coffee, Beth dreading the moment he would have to leave. He had a family, surely, to spend Christmas with.

She felt awkward trying to find out. He wore no alliance, worked alone. He was going again to the resort, to finish his report for the company.

She rose from her chair, all remote gracious hostess.

"Well, it has been a pleasure to have you here," she said, her voice strained.

And how I wish to have you every other night! she thought.

But they were adults. Each leading their own life. Each with their own worries.

"Take care," she said, as he left, his skis slung over his shoulder.

BETH CALLED HER BROTHERS, spoke to her nephews and nieces, a dozen Merry Christmas going and coming over the phone. When you didn't have a family, the gift-giving and other traditions felt trite. She would enjoy some Hallmark movies, cry a bit, and tuck in.

Around midday, Beth went out in the woods behind the house. The forest along her path was sad, all bare branches and tufted dead ferns. She couldn't put Michael out of her head.

A loud crack in the forest made her jump, and she thought of the threat. She crouched behind a wide birch, her left knee flaring at the brusque move.

She looked cautiously. And listened, her heart stammering. Would the mysterious resort owner kill her to get the Inn? Was one or two hapless immigrants roaming the wood?

Would she spend the rest of her life afraid? She sucked in a breath. Her parents had built this dream, and she was not about to let anyone stamp it down.

She rose, to her full five feet two.

"Come on, you bastards! Come get me if you dare!"

Somehow, crying at the top of her lugs felt strangely good. Her voice echoed in the back, the mountain ricocheting her resolve.

She waited out. Nothing.

Other cracks sounded. Beth understood: the temperatures, way below the freezing point, made the sap in the wood snap. She burst out, laughing, for the first time in days, the tension between her shoulders evaporated.

Beth went back in the Inn (that she had left locked). No strange car lurked nearby.

On her balcony, she looked up at the resort, past her poor maples.

Even on this magical day, the activity did not stop.

Happy skiers zigged and zagged down, and she searched a blue outfit. She didn't see it.

Maybe Michael had already left for wherever he had to go.

The night fell, all indigo, on her poor grass.

Her heart heavy, she lit up the Inn's lights display. At least, one Christmas-y thing.

IT WAS when Beth was lighting the candles on the table (set for one) that the call came.

A client? She did not recognize the number. Another threat?

She lifted the landline, apprehensive.

"Beth?" a familiar voice asked.

She was trembling as she said yes.

"I finished my inspection. And I have a Christmas present for you."

Why had he not come here? She could hear a light wind blowing around, he was somewhere outside.

"You should come out on your front gallery."

Beth took the cordless phone with her and unlocked the door.

The Deer Mountain stood, as usual, with its shaved slopes.

Then she heard a loud boom and the familiar hiss of the big war-worthy cannon. Except that the position was a bit angled. She squinted, to check if someone was present. And the plume was odd, too.

What had happened? Where was Michael?

Then she saw it.

Illuminated by the Inn's lights.

Slow, numerous flurries, falling on her lawn. And here it was, at last, her mom's and dad's dream coming true: a magical Christmas

She heard his voice on the phone.

"Do you like it?"

She gasped, couldn't speak.

Michael had aimed the cannon *towards* the inn. Already, snow accumulated on her grass. She didn't care if it was false snow. The crystals shone like diamonds.

"How could you do it?"

"Told you, their employees are not qualified. Their security is a joke. It's a darn miracle no accidents or electrical fire has occurred yet. I went to the control room myself and set the timer, and the cannon position. Child's play."

She smiled, as the white Christmas surrounded her. The roof, the woods, all were covered with the snow, that was real snow.

"Can you come, Michael? I will warm hot chocolate."

The voice answering hers had an echoing quality.

"Didn't I told you I set a timer? I'm right out between your maples!"

And, yes, here he was, standing tall, wearing his smile and blue outfit.

Beth rushed toward him, her bad knee silent for once, her heart already in his welcoming arms.

THEY BROUGHT the mugs to the front couch by the happy Christmas tree, looking at the dark slopes of the resort, now closed for the Holidays. The odd cannon was still putting out snow and would for the night. Michael's report to his company was scathing; the Deer Mountain resort owners would soon have a lot of worries of their own.

Maybe they would need to sell in a hurry. And maybe, Beth thought, some shy deer would return to their mountain.

She sipped the rich hot chocolate spiked with cinnamon, the mug hot under her fingers, with this generous soul that had found her Inn.

Outside, past their reflection, thick snow flurries danced like aerial skiers to cover the landscape.

KATIA AND THE KING RAT

December 24ᵀᴴ, 1968

Katia Illitcha Medveleva, numb and scared, flattened herself against the ground, letting the guard's flashlight beam sweep the air over her.

Soft, fluffy snowflakes draped the trees around her in a fairytale landscape. The flakes tickled her exposed cheek, her numb nose unable to process the smells in that cold. Katia missed the homey scents of the cinnamon *blinis* and the hot spicy chocolate from their hotel, and Olga's gentle smile. She yearned for the warm hotel room she shared with Olga and two other Bolshoi dancers.

Olga, her best friend and confident, blue eyes merry under a cloud of wheat-blond curls that had to be pulled back before she danced as the Sugar Plum Fairy. Olga, whom Katia was leaving behind, feeling like a traitor already.

Sweat streamed under her nylon performer's leotard, forming cold rivulets that the wind made colder, despite the down layer of the parka she had hastily donned. The parka was two sizes too large and even with the belt cinched, she couldn't prevent the icy December air to play inside. She felt wrapped in a frost fence. But the dull mottled brown parka did not draw attention to itself, contrary to her flashy ballet costume, the muslin tutu rustling under the man's blue jeans she wore, also two sizes too large.

The wind that made Katia so cold was an ally. The breeze whistled through the needles of the fir overhead, blurring her traces in the snow as she crossed Oslo's wide Palace Park. She couldn't believe the Royals living in that palace allowed their subjects to walk freely on their property. The streets around the vast park hummed like a tamed beast, Volvos and Citroens flashing by, their drivers intent on returning home.

Katia couldn't return home, ever. That decision was taken as soon as Olga had released her, after a fierce hug, their last. Someone *had* to make sure their absence wouldn't get noticed.

Running away from the Oslo National Theater, creeping through the empty park at night had added to her post-performance exhaustion. Her feet, still in their ballerina shoes, were slowly turning into ice inside the rubber boots she wore. She refrained from breathing out, because a large misty cloud would signal her presence. She waited for the lone guard to recede. A park guardian, not their Securitate.

Her splayed fingers hurt with cold in the red mittens she wore, the melted snow seeping in the damp synthetic fiber.

Olga had given her the mitts minutes after the curtain fell, in the shuffle of performers pulling off tights or resting, the younger girls chattering like happy mice. Everyone else was exhausted, even the Party officer overseeing the last stop of their tour, and his agents who made sure no one strayed far from the herd. The URSS had been rattled when Rudolf Nureyev defected in 1961, while on a tour in Paris. Before him, Nora Kovach and her husband escaped from East Berlin.

Katia's troop tour had started in East Berlin, but the big wall recently built there forbade any try. Their guardian contingent had been pumped up, too, with the rumors of Western spies trying to contact Russian visitors, intent as they were to steal secrets from the URSS Embassy in Oslo.

The Norwegian festivities had distracted their guardian angels, more intent downing capitalist liquors or watching images of the Moon's surface on the TV than checking on their charges.

But this was Christmas night, and there would never be a better time to go, when the whole city rejoiced. Tomorrow morning, an Aeroflot plane would take the troop back to the URSS, and to the powerful *apparatchik* who waited for Katia.

Until ten days ago, Katia had never envisioned being anything else than a ballerina, training and studying and dancing ten hours a day, always supervised, her calories intake counted, even when every muscle in her legs clamored for rest. Katia never balked under the harsh comment of the choreographer, she thrived in the effort, as she coveted the lofty title of Prima ballerina. The Moscow press had praised her talent in the last *Giselle* ballet and her oval face was spread far and wide.

The flowers had started coming then. More and more bouquets, coming from a high-placed Party member Katia had met at the ballroom of the Bolshoi, for a reception.

I love your pure talent, he had said.

She winced at the memory, her empty stomach burning inside.

To distract her mind from the fear, she looked up at the Moon's bright sickle glowing through the weaving branches. The USA had sent a rocket with men in space, to go around the Moon in time for this special night. She had heard on the radio one American astronaut call for *peace on all of you on this good Earth*, a sentence Olga had translated for her.

Katia doubted there would be any peace if the URSS did not impose it to the rest of this *good Earth*.

~

TEN PACES in front of Katia, the dancer who had found her both the pants and the parka was hugging the ground, still wearing his costume, minus the ridiculous cylindrical Nutcracker hat. Lev's nylon outfit flashed like a Christmas decorations, lime green and carmine. (The Bolshoi's colorful and bold approach to dance competed with the pure classicism of St. Petersburg's Kirov Company. Nevertheless, the rival school had, in 1892, been the first one to present the Nutcracker ballet to the world.)

"The embassy is just on the other side of that park, Kat," Lev said.

Levi Bronstein and Katia had jumped from a second-story window, together like doomed lovers, even if they were neither lovers nor doomed, except if they stayed. Hand in hand for stability, landing in the soft snow, their dancer's legs easily absorbing the shock. A last look, Olga's pale oval watching over them like an angel.

The park had been empty as they ran in, but they avoided the wide paths and the guardians. Lev, Jewish, handsome and fresh-faced, suffered from his unnatural (so the Party said) attraction to his own sex, an act that could get him a seat in a Siberia-bound prisoner train. As he was aware of her own predicament, he had made plans to escape with her.

Come to my datcha, the Party member had purred at the last reception, showing a range of perfect, white teeth, his fat fingers feeling the hard curve of her leg under her tutu.

Katia was fine-boned and short, with a slender grace that belied her twenty years. That child-like grace had propelled Katia into the coveted role of Clara, but it had also drawn the attention of some well-established men belonging to the *Nomenklatura*. Meaning, untouchable.

The young dancer shivered, thinking about the Party member who so evoked the King Rat of the play. Oh, that King Rat had no difficulty convincing talented girls to spend some time in his datcha. The director couldn't say *niet* to this high-powered *apparatchik*. This had gone on for years, so some girls knew about the attention lavished on them, and the danger.

The last ballerina invited at the datcha had been her Olga, with her full bosom and her wheat-blond hair. Already, her belly was ballooning; it would be a matter of days before the troop director noticed her pregnancy and sent her packing back to her rigid family in Smolensk.

Katia knew she was next on the man's *tableau de chasse*. Once the plane landed in Moscow. His creepy way of saying she was the best Clara he had ever seen.

I love your pure talent.

Katia loved ballet, but she could never go back once that King Rat apparatchik had his way with her. But refusing outright was dangerous. Favors could transform into punishments. Katia hadn't been wise in her reaction, stepping away from the groping hands. That had only excited the King Rat.

I will wait for your return, malyshka.

Little girl. The director would not look Katia in the eye.

Once they finished this European tour, the *apparatchik* would be waiting at the airport, with a special limousine. Katia's pious mother would never look at her in the eyes, after the man forced her. Even if atheism was the official religion, many remnants of the Christian faith perdured.

"We're not far," Lev said.

The guards' silhouettes receded towards the lighted avenue. Even in the distance, they could hear the joyous carols and loud cheers of the free civilians.

Katia's hopes rose. They should be far enough from the Opera house.

Would the Party overseer renounce? Was he also expecting a bribe from the powerful apparatchik?

"Stop!" a Russian-accented voice shouted.

Katia's heart thumped like a mad horse's hooves. They had been discovered! Of course, the first places the armed Securitate guards would look would be the embassies. Had not Rudolf Nureyev stayed behind in 1961? His defection at the end of a tour had shocked the politburo.

Lev rolled over himself and pushed the heavy bag on her. He pointed at the crenellated peaked roof of the Canadian Embassy, two streets away.

"Go, now! I will draw them away."

"But..."

He winced, his Nutcracker make up cracking. Then he smiled, this infectious smile she loved.

"Your King Rat's not interested in boys. Now, run!"

Before she could protest, Lev jumped, doing a perfect *entrechat*, and took off in the opposite direction. It was too late to run after him.

She heard shouts, then the summons. A loud, angst-filled laugh rose under the indifferent stars, cut by a lone gun shot.

Lev!

Dying for her, like the Nutcracker battling the King of Rats.

Katia's legs bounced almost without her being conscious she was moving, erupting from the trees into the street, her ungainly boots tapping loud on the cleared path. She shucked them off, preferring to run on her faithful pointe shoes, perfectly bound to her ankles. She felt the moisture seep up from the thick hide sole, but at least she was silent as a fairy, the rolled jeans not hindering her moves.

She pictured Lev's lean body riddled by bullets. No magic would bring him from death... She discarded the heavy parka as she ran, keeping only his shoulder bag with the money and cards inside. The mittens, too damp, had to go, too.

The street was filled with cars and people hurrying to and from candy-colored shops, none who would care about an underage fugitive.

One street only, only one street. Her dance shoes tapped the powdery sidewalks as she weaved around revelers. One rail-thin man reeking of alcohol, tried to catch her, maybe seeing her as an apparition.

As she swerved to avoid his hands, Katia left foot slipped on a patch of dark ice. She landed hard on one elbow, while the drunk emitted a harsh laugh behind her, rejoicing in her fall.

"You OK?" another voice asked, younger, and female.

Strong hands helped her up, the leather gloves soft against her bare hands. When Katia looked up, she met two cerulean-blue eyes under a fringe of blond hair so much like Olga's she gasped aloud.

The stranger wore an angel-white knitted bonnet and a rich, fruity perfume that reminded her of strawberries. A dark blue coat fell to her ankles and smelled of old wool. She had an expressive, heart-shaped face like a benevolent Sugar Plum fairy, and lips as red as a ripe cherry. But those generous lips stretched with concern as she looked Katia up, undone black chignon and frost-covered leotard and tutu emerging from the jeans' waistband.

"Oh, poor child, you'll freeze to death! Take this!"

Katia didn't understand the woman's accented English, but she got the gist of it when the stranger plunked her knitted cap on Katia's snow-brushed hair.

The move unloosened a wealth of golden hair, so soft Katia wished she had time to touch the silken strands. The woman was unbuttoning her long coat –too long for the ballerina's smaller size, but there was a knitted cardigan under that...—when shouts echoed at the intersection.

"*Spasibo*," she said, and took off like a hare.

Katia barely heard the *yourewelcome* the fairy-looking Westerner uttered after her. More shouts in Russian cut the air behind her, *found her*!

The woman's voice rose, talking too fast for Katia to understand, but there was no missing the groan that interrupted her discourse.

The brutality shocked Katia. She itched to look behind her, but, no, she couldn't, not now. At least, they couldn't fire in the crowded street.

She ran, each step as painful as the Andersen's human-transformed mermaid would have felt. The peaked roof of the Embassy shone like a beacon, topped by the flag featuring a red maple leaf.

Lev and she had studied the map of the district around the Opera house. They had considered the US Embassy, but Olga had said it was too far, and that it would be the first place their guardians would look. Instead, they had settled for the less-obvious Canadian one. Lev had proposed asking shelter from a church, but there was no guarantee they would not end up in the Securitate hands.

Cold air hit Katia's back and neck, sending more shivers.

One half street to go.

She heard distant shouts behind her.

This was her chance. Instead of making for the carved grid of the entrance, she aimed for the right side. The wall was higher that a man's height, but she sped up, drawing alarmed shouts from the pursuing guards. *Stop! Stop!*

Katia concentrated the last of her strength for a powerful leap. Her fingers grabbed the wall's top. She needed to take a breather, arms and lungs in fire. But she couldn't wait for the men to aim their rifles at her uncovered back. And the big white hat felt like a shining target...

Talent scouts recruited gymnasts as well as dancers. Katia had had a gymnastic training at the start, the two disciplines requesting a healthy amount of stamina. She called back her body's ingrained knowledge and, toes and knees scraping the concrete, anchored an arm over the top and heaved her small weight over the top.

All this time, she expected a bullet to end her escape. The shouts melted in the background of car engines, and more people were shouting as well, a hail of *Merry Christmas* and *God Bless you* that would be an insult in comrade Brejnev's URSS.

The broken glass shards jutting from the wall cut her shoulders and arms, but she planted her palms between the cutting edges and vaulted over the obstacle, as gracefully as a rehearsed performance.

THE EMBASSY PEOPLE were amiable and gave Katia not only shelter, but the joy of eating and celebrating a western Christmas. At twenty, she was still underage, but Olga had skillfully forged her passport six days ago to make her five months older.

The next night, she was on a plane to Montréal, as a political refugee, to be processed.

On that Christmas night, as the Boeing 707 left the airport, her only possession was a pearly-white knitted cap, with a name, *Helen*, embroidered on the lining.

KATIA'S TRIALS were far from magically over once she crossed the Atlantic. It marked the start of a labyrinth of administrative worries and practical consideration.

Languages was not her strong suit, but she had to learn English. Olga's forgery was eventually discovered. As an underage, Katia couldn't ask for shelter, a fact that the King Rat and the Politburo envoy used to force the Canadian authorities to release Katia.

However, one thing Canadians were good at was to make the procedures last. They lasted long enough that, on the spring of 1969, Katia reached the magical age of 21 years and found herself mistress of her own destiny.

Her parents were severely blamed for their daughter's actions.

Immigrants generally had a hard time in a new country, and Katia expected no less. So she was surprised in the summer of 1969 when her immigration agent told Katia that a trust fund had been set in her name, from an anonymous donor. She could study the arts and establish herself in any province, once she became a naturalized citizen.

Katia quickly adapted to the milder Canadian winters, often wearing the white knitted cap. She had never been able to find out about that mysterious Helen living in Oslo. The cap had been obviously handmade by a doting mother or grandmother.

In the following years, Katia wrote many letters to her parents, but the Iron Curtain gobbled them up. Had they moved from their Moscow flat? Had they been exiled to a Siberian camp? Were they dead, like Lev? And her dear friend Olga? She would be a mother by now.

The soft knitted cap helped her remember that there was some good in humanity.

Toronto, December 24th, 1992

The Christmas Eve Nutcracker Charity ball was the third Katia had helped set up for the National Ballet of Canada.

She taught technique in ballet school, using methods developed by masters like Ludmilla Chiriaeff, founder of the *Grand Ballets Canadiens*. Katia's method upheld a teaching respectful of each student's capacities. The training was still grueling, but no psychological abuse, no draconian diet, no unsavory competition was imposed on the young ones. What a change from her former life...

More and more, her spirit drifted to her homeland, in such throes. Now that the URSS was no more (and who knew what would follow?) she wished she had news.

She couldn't believe how much the world had changed since she had settled in Canada. The past year had seen the dislocation of the old URSS, with fifteen Soviet Republics leaving the nest.

While she waited behind the curtains for her own character's entrance. Katia passed her hands on her muslin costume. Over her head, rows of mirrored globe lights shattered any shadow.

The O'Keefe Center for Performing Arts looked like an architect's dream. It had none of the out-of-this-world eccentricity of the Royal Thompson Hall (that evoked a landed UFO), nor had it the dignity and majesty of the Moscow's Bolshoi Theater. Nevertheless, the Torontonian architects had cared about disabled performers and guests, making the place accessible to wheelchairs.

And the O'Keefe Centre had perfect acoustics. The National Ballet of Canada had spared nothing to make this Nutcracker's performance a memorable experience. The young and not-so-young public had been carried with enthusiasm by the orchestra play, while the story of Clara and the Nutcracker unfolded on stage. The winter had conspired, too, with a soft fall of big snowflakes making the skyscrapers and the CN tower phantomatic.

Katia did not play Clara, of course, but dancing had kept her slender and fit, enough to allow her to participate in the charity event performance, even in her forties. Tonight, she would dance as a delicate Sugar Plum fairy. Her breath caught.

Olga's role, on that last night...

"Penny for your thoughts?" a voice asked, the French accent undeniable.

Lost in her thoughts, Katia turned.

The King Rat stood, holding his big furry head in his hands.

Like her, Luc Casgrain was an older dancer, chosen for the charity performance, doing the King Rat's part. He had good-humor wrinkles and a ready smile, and four adorable children. One of the girls showed promise, and Katia trained her herself. Luc Casgrain was a good man, Katia liked him very much, but she preferred to avoid relationships.

Lev and Olga. Too many sad memories were attached to this Christmas Eve.

"Oh, I miss my friends home," she said.

He sighed.

"Yes, like I miss Deanna," he said.

His wife had been snatched by cancer four years ago.

"But I'm sure the situation will improve," he said. "The Cold War's behind us, so..."

But Katia shook her head, not trusting her voice.

Upheavals had never brought good things in her old homeland.

"You never talk about your life, before," he said.

Because she felt guilty, not having tried harder to find what happened to her friends. She never talked about her escape, more than twenty years ago. Luc shifted besides her, a benevolent presence. She would have loved to hold him, but the first bars of the score echoed in the perfect acoustic of the O'Keefe Theater.

And Katia let herself be wrapped like a happy parcel in the magic of Nutcracker.

Dancing. Dancing helped her forget anything.

She loved all the performers, especially this new King Rat, who was currently occupied dancing against the Nutcracker. The practices had made the performance perfect. She couldn't see the public, but the fan-shaped room held about a thousand seats.

Katia floated through the Tchaikovsky suite, with her partners. Her welcoming of Clara and her prince, then her *Pas de deux* with her own Prince... And then, the Sugar Plum fairy and her prince danced off the scene, and she waited until the young Clara left in a make-believe sleight.

When all the dancers assembled for the final bow, she caught a glance of fairy tale eyes in the first row. But no, this was an illusion brought by the light contrast. And the curtain fell.

The King Rat hefted his false furry head under one arm.

"Now, I guess it's time for the second part."

THE ARTIFICIAL TREE WAS HUGE, a size which obliged everyone to step around the pile of presents.

Katarina had showered as fast as she could, to join the rest of the Nutcracker cast in the vast hall. The place was built for great events, and this would be one well-attended... by the Canadian government's own *apparatchiks*.

She checked her gown, modest in a dark red tone that matched her lipstick color, setting off her teeth when she smiled. And, at those times, she had a lot to smile about. The Charity event had been a success. The budding computer technologies had spread the word far and wide.

Well-dressed guests were milling about, while the minister of culture expounded on the importance of the arts. Katia stood by the tall tree, whose red and green lights blinked haphazardly. Children were playing in a special corner, while their parents, who had paid a high fee to watch the performance, talked in small powerful groups.

On the buffet table, festive food assemblages screamed *eat me*! in various colors, and she had sampled the fruitcake and delicate almond cookies.

She felt tired, not exactly happy, but satisfied with her efforts. Her coat and white cap waited for her, on a chair by the windows, where the snow played with the city's lights.

She could go, now. They did not need her presence anymore, and several of her companions had hit the buffet table.

One of the ubiquitous servers planted a ball of red wine (that matched her gown) before she had the reflex to protest that no, she didn't drink.

She looked around to find a table to leave her wine glass when a woman's voice called.

"Miss Medveleva?"

Something was eerily familiar, but she couldn't replace it. Katia pivoted.

And almost crushed the slight stem of the glass, the liquid dancing.

Luc, dashing in his irreproachable smoking and his real salt-and-pepper hair, was standing next to a middle-aged woman in a blooming-green dress, her thin shoulders wrapped under a knitted shawl. Her bony hand clutched the head of a delicate bamboo cane. A shiny black purse hung from her spotted shoulder by a spaghetti-thin strap. The silver hair bounced in delicate curls, but it was the eyes, those large, sky-blue eyes that projected reassurance.

The gaze fastened on the soft wool of the cap laid on the chair.

"You kept it."

Katia didn't recognize any individual traits, all entered her consciousness at the same time with a faint, delicate strawberry scent.

It was her! Her mysterious Oslo angel.

Helen.

THE ANGEL HAD MORE lines around the eyes now and was stooped, but Katia did not mind a bit. In the background, the children had pounced on the presents at the base of the giant tree. Their excited shrieks and the soft tearing sound of the silky wrapping paper added to the hum of conversations.

"You!" she said, flabbergasted. "It was you!"

"Mrs. Helen Bonin is one of our donators," Luc said, a mild surprise in his expressive eyes.

"And my most important investment was this young girl," the woman said. "I'm happy I to meet you, at last!"

Investment? A second later, the lightbulb flashed in her mind. The funds. The mysterious funds.

"But, how did you know me? I never gave you my name, I was just..."

Scared out of my wits. Fleeing.

Helen shrugged.

"Well, that ballet outfit you wore, the security beefed up around the Theater, and all those Nutcracker posters across the city... I put two and two together."

Luc motioned them to a table.

"I don't have my legs of before," she said, sinking with relish in the padded chair. "Even then, I couldn't run after those horrid men, child. Bad knee."

"Were you a resident in Oslo?"

"Hah! I was just another tourist enjoying the *sand-bakkels* and butter cookies."

"What did you do?"

"Your daring escape made the local news, and I contacted the Embassy. Alas, they had already put you on a plane."

Helen let out a sigh, her fingers working the shawl.

"I couldn't go to Canada because of my job, a ten-year contract near Helsinki. But I traced your name and send monies to your immigration agent so you could live well, and get a degree. All through the Oslo Embassy."

Katia felt like a child deprived of her present.

"Then, why didn't you contact me?" she asked.

There was a catch, a half-second of pause.

"I couldn't at the time. Not in my line of work. It would have been... a *faux-pas*."

Katia sensed something hidden in Helen's answer.

"When I came back to Canada, you had moved out of Montréal, and this time I lost your trace. I only found where you actually were this summer."

Helen cast a look at Luc.

"Could you get me a glass of water, dear?"

The tall Rat King nodded, a twinkle of amusement in his eye. When he left, Helen spoke on a low tone.

"Because, now that I am retired from the RCMP, and reasonably affluent, I *can* help you."

The Royal Canadian Mounted Police was quite well-known body that doubled as an intelligence service.

"Your work... Were you... a spy?"

"In Helsinki, near the Russian border."

Katia felt her eyes go wide.

"Really?"

Helen tapped her left knee under the dress.

"No James Bond shenanigans, my dear. I was an observer and a courier, which is dangerous enough, as my poor knee can attest. And I was *really* vacationing when I met this scared young fugitive."

Katia inclined her head, looking at the bank of windows behind their seats, the snowflakes set off by the yellow exterior lights like an infinity of phantoms.

"You said you can help me?"

"I worked with what you told your immigration agent. It took time, but I retraced your parents."

Katia sucked in a lungful of air. She felt suddenly hot, and thirsty.

"Mom, Dad?"

Katia leaned forward on her chair.

"You have their address?"

"Better than that."

Helen opened her shiny leather purse with a loud snap. She pulled off an envelope, its paper crinkled by the transit, one corner torn, with a flashy red and blue Perestroika stamp on the right corner. The envelope was addressed to

Helen, at a Montréal, QC address. The return address was in the Urals.

Katia recognized the nervous, angular handwriting of her mother, the ball point pen almost piercing the paper.

"That's your first Christmas gift," Helen said. "The Perestroika allowed them to write."

She let her fingers roam on the crinkled paper, felt the corners bend when she applied delicate pressure, as if her mom's soul resided inside... She resisted the urge to tear the precious letter open.

"My first Christmas gift?" she said. "Does that mean there's another one?"

Helen's angel-like smile stretched her thinner lips. Oh, Katia guessed how good this woman had been at her line of not-James-Bond work.

The ex-spy raised her head, beaming.

"Here they are!" she said. "Good thing this place is accessible."

Katia heard the metal creaks of a wheelchair. She turned to meet Helen's companions.

At first, she didn't recognize the bearded man in the wheelchair, wearing a simple black turtleneck and blue jeans. But he obviously did, his face beaming as those brown eyes and mischievous grin had stayed the same.

"You haven't changed a bit, Kat."

"L-LEV?" she said, in a gasp. "Is that you?"

The man snorted, in that familiar way when speaking of the *apparatchiks*.

"It sure is, cause he's heavy enough!" another voice said.

Katia's attention swiveled to the stately, fortyish woman pushing the wheelchair. That voice, changed, but oh-so-familiar, melted something inside her.

The wheat-blond hair had become a ginger-colored mane, and the make-up made her oval face look thinner, but the blue eyes had never changed. And that long blue dress, the neckline opening like a flower, complemented her generous frame.

"O, Olga?"

The blue eyes filled with mirth.

"I'm not a ghost, either!"

"This is your other Christmas gift," Helen Bonin said. "My colleagues in the service owed me a few favors. It took some time to trace your friends. They went through a lot."

"And *that* story would take all night," Lev said.

Katia crouched in front of the man, taking his hands in hers.

"What you did, then, you paid for it..."

He snorted, displaying again this impish smile under his graying hair.

"They were lousy shots, Kat. Took one bullet in the leg. But I was sent in exile for eight years, then I managed to cross the Finnish border. That (he showed the wheelchair) happened in California, a rock-climbing accident."

Katia turned to Olga.

"My story's more complicated. I carried the corrupt apparatchik's child, but my family had the baby quickly adopted away because, oh, the scandal!

She whipped the air with both hands.

"I became a dance teacher in Smolensk, got married, lost my man to one of the stupid wars the Soviets lit up in Africa. When the Berlin Wall fell, I decided that was it, said bye-bye to my uppity family, and crossed the lines with a few others. Helen found me because I kept asking for you in the Finnish Canadian Embassy."

"We landed in Toronto last week," Lev said.

That's when Luc rounded the wheelchair and deposited two glasses of fizzling water on the table.

"I brought one for you, Kat. This place is so dry it makes anyone thirsty. Huh, hello, did you appreciate the ballet?" he asked Lev, all amiable hospitality.

"He's the King Rat," Katia said, deadpan.

Olga's shoulders shook, and Lev spluttered, while Katia took a cautious swallow of fresh water. The water did more than sate her thirst, it carried away like a river the load of worry from Katia's mind.

"I really prefer *this* King Rat!" Lev said.

"Can someone explain me what's so funny?" Luc asked, his brows lifted in puzzlement.

Katia rose, feeling light as a feather. She grabbed the King Rat's hands, which surprised both of them.

"The friends I thought lost forever, they're here!" she said, as excited as the children squabbling by the tree.

Helen cleared her throat, as Lev rolled closer to his and Olga's benefactress.

"Well, *my child*, you've waited long enough for your gift."

Katia smiled, tears streaming along her face and spotting her gown as she let go of Luc's hands.

Olga looked regal in that blue flowing dress, her face lit up from inside, as Katia's must be, too. Their friendship burnt like powerful, healing sun.

As Katia, at long last, walked in her friend's arms, she felt the Sugar Plum Fairy had bever left.

HOLY, JAZZY NIGHT

THIS CITY DOESN'T LIKE me, Felia thought as she hurried through Bloor & Yonge, taking advantage of the four-direction pedestrian lights. The white walker light figures on all corners switched for the red hand sign, blinking, but she pressed on, hoping to gain a few seconds.

She was taking a chance crossing Toronto's largest intersection, loaded as she was with her Christmas presents, but she was sick of the weather, as if the worst offsprings of the Water family had decided to play havoc with the city. The isolated episodes of light, fluffy snow of the morning had morphed into a full-scale model of when *Hell freezes over*. And the skyscrapers aligned on Bloor Avenue formed a wind corridor that the rain was only too happy to play in.

She launched herself, eyes slitted against incoming ice pellets that added themselves to the wet snow, both transforming the shiny asphalt in a thick porridge of melted snow and mud, reeking of fuel exhaust and calcite salt. Her pale green coat was getting heavier as rain lodged in the woolen fabric.

This year's winter Solstice was the worst, ever. Pedestrians were dark ghosts disappearing in the storm.

Then, just as the hand on the pedestrian streetlight stopped blinking, the heel of her left ankle boot snapped open, changing her equilibrium equation on the slippery ground. Felia and her bags took a graceless plunge in the soot-tainted slush. Her bad hand opened, releasing the bags.

The shock reverberated in her knees, ill-protected by the layer of thin fabric. The pain flared as a loud screech of brakes and a blaring horn concert rose behind her. By luck, she hadn't broken a finger, but her palms hurt through her thin gloves.

She looked up at the radiator grid of a red low-riding Carfati sports sedan. She couldn't see the driver, but she knew, she just knew O Lord, that this sports car driver had punched the accelerator split seconds *before* his own light turned green. Her ex had driven that kind of rocket-sports cars to events...

The horn continued to wail, a reminder of how a mere pedestrian didn't belong there in Carland.

Of course, Ophelia, carrying four large bags of candies and goodies for her nephew, had chosen that moment to slip right in front of the driver. More cars joined the fray, tooting in an ear-grating disharmony, drivers gunning their engines in an angry rumble, all itching to run her over. A part of her was reminded of the klaxon concert in *An American in Paris*, but a less happy version.

She skittered low on the ground, on her aching knees. Several emotions competed for her attention: fear of dying then and there, anger at the recklessness of the Carfati driver, sorrow for her little nephew who would not get his treats, ache from her mistreated knee, anger – again! — because, yes, her pants were ruined.

She clawed around, clutching at bag handles and odd-shaped goodies boxes. One bag had slid toward the very center of the intersection, disgorging its contents, more wrapped boxes and a colorful slew of marble-sized wrapped chocolates. She bent over to grab the stray bag and one box, keeping the other bag handles in her good right hand. Her left couldn't close in a fist to save her life.

A whoosh of air rustled through her coat when the Carfati swerved around her, its extra-large tires — made for racing, not commuting— sliding a few inches before the unseen driver punched the mud in a straight line. Drops of that same mud landed on her, finishing her good coat. She heard a snarky line about her anatomy, but the window rolled over before she could get a glimpse of the guy.

Not waiting for the other road crazies to follow the Carfati, Felia scrambled like mad in the thickening caramel-toned slush to reach the curb. Her feet were freezing. Her fancy boots were now thoroughly drenched, and certainly dying from the calcium salt overdose.

Her eyes stung with tears, she collided with an icy streetlamp base, a newspaper distributor with sharp angles which pulled a curse from her lips, and a warm leather wall that enfolded her like a soft armor.

The near-fatal encounter had left her so stunned that her first reflex was to look back at the intersection. A groan escaped her as she watched the pink, perfect, pricey chocolate marbles roll and die under the tires of rushing cars.

Then she became conscious of the leather. A coat, belonging to someone taller than she was, arms pressing gently on her shoulders. The touch felt both strong and reassuring, not two qualities she often saw linked. Her cheek pressed against the opening of the coat, she smelled a discreet Cologne scent mixed with the clean odor of soap and moist wool. She closed her eyes and lingered, a scant few seconds, in this unexpected, protective embrace.

She heard a voice, a soothing, low-register murmur laden with concern.

"It's okay, now, but please, don't try to get the rest of your things!"

She blinked. She had heard that voice before, but where? And when? She shifted, and the arms that had enclosed her opened like petals.

Felia lifted her head to the stranger.

Her gaze met a pair of vivacious eyes the color of her grandma's mahogany desk, a straight nose, a generous mouth, the jaw ringed by a short, well-kept beard that showed a few white threads. He was probably in his late thirties, a few years older than she was. His jutting cheekbones gave his face a harmonious hexagon shape. His hair spilled in unruly curls from his bonnet. The man towered over her, looking like a *coureur des bois* mixed with Bob Marley.

When he smiled, his teeth sparkled in his brown face, the skin one tone lighter than his eyes. He was looking down at her, his traits modelled in a kind expression.

She felt a warm rush in her cheeks, little electric fleas running over her scalp. The freezing rain, the city and the cars, the blinking lights and gaudy decorations, were muffled.

Felia did not believe in 'LAFS', as her older niece liked to spout among many obscure teenager's acronyms. The daughter of an Ontarian kinder garden teacher and an exiled Haitian journalist, she wore the scars of a dozen bad relationships, the last one ended four years ago. She was not about to enter another whirlwind roller-coaster that would leave her broken again...

But.

In a moment, the handsome stranger would go back his way, and she hers. But now, just now, oh please Lord, make this *now* last forever! She would treasure this moment for the rest of her life.

THE BUBBLE BURST, pierced by a ringtone arpeggio. His phone. The man's smile vanished, replaced by a frown, a shadow in his eyes.

Back to the real world.

"Oh, yes, I'll be OK," she said in a hurry, not wanting to keep this gentle man away from his duties, or from his family? "Thanks for, er, being there."

He slipped one huge hand in a pant's pocket and silenced the phone's mid-ring. Not even consulting the screen. "It's just the usual," he said, but a set of lines appeared on his temple.

Felia brushed off the mud adhering to her nylon pants. Which left a brown, smelly smudge over her knees, the humidity seeping through the light fabric and coating her helpless kneecaps. As she took a step away from the bubble, a sharp pain flared on her left knee.

She bit her lips to avoid crying out, but he must have seen her wince.

"You're hurt," he said, brown knitted together.

The concern she read in his eyes looked genuine. But she didn't want him to see the old scar that ran up her shin and plagued her knee.

"I, I just took a spill," she said, one hand covering her knee.

Suddenly, she felt acutely conscious of her dirty clothes, her less-than perfect teeth. He bent over and grabbed the handles of the bunch of bags, his gloved hand brushing her free arm.

"Let's go over there. There's a café I know, and at least you'll be warm."

She let him guide her to one of the tall buildings erected to harbor the growing business sector. The entrance doors were protected by a curved steel-and-aluminum overhang that looked like a spaceship hull. As soon as they passed out of the rain, she felt better.

As she did minutes later, breathing in the wonderful aroma of a mug of latté, cupped between her hands to draw more warmth. She must have been really tired to let someone else pay for her. Somewhere along, in the fog of exhaustion, she had released her name.

"Ophelia? It's a rare, poetic name," he said, taking the seat in front of their plate-sized table. "'I'm Timothy."

She felt relieved he hadn't asked, like so many others, if she had a brother named Laerte.

"I prefer Felia," she said. "My mother was a Shakespeare fan. Still is."

The upholstered bench felt warm on her back. She sat cross-legged, because her boots were drying over a hot air vent. Her coat draped on the chair was dripping on the tiled floor, but the barista didn't mind. The place was small, and oddly intimate for such a building. The intersection circus and the cold were on the other side of the glass window.

A soft jazz song played in background. She recognized the little-girl high-pitched voice of Blossom Dearie. Then, a piano piece, arpeggios mounting and falling, like a boogie-woogie. She would never play as well...

"Is this from Mary Lou Williams?" she asked.

Mary Lou Williams had started playing at five, and had a perfect ear. But like many women in music, her compositions had been ignored for decades, only revived in the 90s. Felia had played two of her pieces in a recital at her school.

He turned, his eyes unfocused. Then he nodded.

"Yup. One of her early comps, *Roll On*."

This time the warm tingle ran all over her mind. She had not met anyone so knowledgeable, outside jazz musicians.

"They like to play jazz here."

"One of the reasons I come here," he said.

His phone beeped. This time, he glanced at the screen. His lips pressed in a thin line.

"Well, when I'm not at work," he said, putting the phone back in the pocket.

But Felia could see his mood plain on his features. Something was gnawing at him. A wife trying to call? A boss? Some of her happy juice leaked out. Was she, again, falling for the wrong guy?

"Here's your cappu', mister Tim," the young man said

in a bouncy voice. Then he grinned. "I'm looking forward to your next broadcast."

Tim took a sip of his cappuccino, eyes closed in obvious relish. He deposited the porcelain cup without a single *clink*. Those fingers were delicate, even if they were as thick as the pattern of his cream knit sweater.

"So, do you work at the radio?" she asked.

He nodded.

"Oh, I wondered how you could recognize a Mary Lou Williams piece."

"I used to host a late-evening jazz program, on CBC."

"Do you still do?"

Again, the cloud in his eyes.

"It got cancelled last year. Budget cuts."

His voice had plunged to a lower, deeper register as he delivered the curt answer.

Felia blinked, and like a switch, her memories came back.

HER LAST BOYFRIEND had been a talented jazz saxophonist and pianist. Zoomer, he called himself. Six years ago, she had auditioned as a pianist for his band, *Sick Talents,* in a bar. He had been enraptured by her talent. And by her classical looks, like a modern Mary Lou Williams, he had said, which pleased her to no end.

They had embraced each other, not a whirlwind

romance: a tornado of passions, playing all night on various instruments.

She moved in his loft, bringing her enthusiasm and her small, straight-backed Yamaha. Birthing music from the touch of finger pads on piano keys was a magical wonder.

She helped him any way she could, putting up placards on walls, making cold calls. She had joined the band, but money was tight, and she had a roof anyway, didn't she? She accompanied them on piano, also doing the back vocals when the band performed in clubs. Many appreciated seeing a brown woman in the group.

She should have left, then, should have noticed Zoomer's and his band buddies' occasional drinking. But she was in love. And he was paying the sky-high Toronto rent on the loft.

So Felia powered on, playing for smiles, thinking about Mary Lou Williams growing up in the late 1920s and 1930s. Williams, a strong-willed musician, had also been an unpaid pianist, and 'arranger' for her band. Meaning, she adapted existing pieces into parts played by all instruments of a band, a demanding work. And she composed, too, but her own pieces would come to light much later.

Two years into their story, Felia's beau's 'occasional' drinking had morphed into a binge every evening, where his friends smoked and guzzled liters of cheap wine. Their relation soured.

One night before Christmas, she gathered the courage to ask him to be paid for her playing, like the others in the band. Zoomer got red in the face. He shouted his heart out, about how he felt betrayed, how she was no more than a talentless gold-digger.

Then he stomped out, slamming the door behind him. Going drinking, again.

Felia found herself alone in the vast loft, on Christmas Eve of all days, huddling over her bruised soul.

The radio was playing a beloved piece by Diana Krall, a Canadian who played piano like a queen. And Luis Armstrong's take on *White Christmas*. After the soothing jazz, the program host's deep, rich voice had led her elsewhere, presenting more healing music.

That same night, Felia ran out to her sister Lucy, who lived in North York. The weather was terrible. She slipped, landing on her knee and hands on the icy sidewalk. The crashed knee was nothing, but her left annular and auricular joints hurt so much she knew they were broken.

Her fingers eventually healed, but her ring finger joint was askew. She couldn't close her fist properly. She got her small piano back from Zoomer, with the help of Lucy and her husband. But she could not get herself to play on it again.

The following year, Felia had kept listening to the program hosted by Timothy Dickson, until the season ended. Then life happened: she sold her Yamaha, took new studies in tech, hunted for menial jobs.

Until now.

Felia felt another flush roam through her whole body,

or maybe it was her poor abused legs finally getting some warmth.

"I'm sorry about that," she managed to say.

He let out a rumbling chuckle that reminded her of ice cubes clicking inside a drink.

"Hey, that's called life. But I have an evening program on Jazz FM 91. This week, I co-host the Christmas Specials. The next broadcast is airing tonight, at nine."

Felia was about to ask if he played an instrument, but he came up with a question of his own.

"And you, what do you do when not running in the traffic?"

"I, well, I work at a restaurant," she said.

A burst of shame rose in her like a bubble of hot, methane gas. She added: "for now." She couldn't tell this nice man about the string of bad decisions and debts that had landed her to make ends meet by working as a Thai restaurant counter.

"And, if I may be so bold, what do you want to do, after *now*?"

"I, I don't know. But when I come into some savings, I will buy more music. My favorites are..."

Tim listened, his dark eyes and attention focused on her. The table felt small and smaller as an electrical tension built between them. She didn't know if he sang of played, but he was a keen listener. As she talked about piano, and jazz, her hands were flying by themselves.

"You do have a pianist's hands," he said.

Very softly, so as not to scare her, he took her left hand between his. The contact sent more tingling through her fingers.

"I'm not talented."

His eyes widened at the promptness of her response. She had answered by reflex. Felia had believed, a long time ago, that she had talent. But she had not touched a piano since she sold her Yamaha.

Now, his eyes fell on her twisted annular, but he did not remark on it.

"So, you played, before," he said.

She felt about to cry out: *no more*. But his warm radio host voice prodded gently.

So, drinking from a refilled cup, Felia told him how she played piano as a child, inspired by the dexterity of jazzmen and -women. She had planned to study music, but the student debts sank her after two years. She had a closet-sized Yamaha for practice. She glossed over her failed relationships, saying that she had tried (and failed) to enter the jazz scene. Eventually, her small Yamaha had to go to pay her new studies in electronics.

Her voice caught as she talked. Her right hand brushed over her left, in a reflex.

"You sold your piano?" Tim said, his brows raising almost to his hairline.

"I couldn't keep it and pay the rent."

She had registered in a promising technical college, costly. A Hi-tech joint hired her, but went belly-up when a competitor got a lower-quality process accepted as a new standard.

"Techno start-ups. I can relate to that," he said.

He suddenly frowned. She heard the muffled buzzing of his phone set on vibration.

"You must be popular. Your phone never stops ringing."

He stretched his lips in a half-smile, like a theatrical figure, sad and joyous at the same time.

"That's no admirers," he said. "It's my band of hecklers. My superiors at the station often dispute my choices, especially if we feature too many Black or female artists. But those trolls have gotten hold of my phone number, and they send hateful messages, to me and my crew."

"They, they want you out?"

"They dream of it. Even my co-host had been threatened."

The phone buzzed, again. Felia nodded a silent OK. He lowered his eyes on the screen. She feared another heckler message, but his luminous smile returned.

"That's Brigit, my co-host. I'm about to be late at the studio."

TIM WALKED with her to the subway station. She felt at ease, his presence providing a shield against both the weather and tourists drunk on Holiday Season Specials.

Tim had purchased a sturdy reuse bag at a small shop near the café, where her flimsy paper bags fit nicely.

The rain had abated, leaving sparkling snow coating the walkways, which mirrored the red and green lights of the department store's windows. A soft snow started falling, fluffy flurries that she could catch on her tongue.

It was another beautiful bubble moment, as they commented on the Christmas store decorations. She noted how Tim was as generous to the homeless sleeping under the gaudy windows, leaving two golden dollars in the upturned cap of one. How such a man could still be alone was impossible.

The subway entrance came too fast.

"Felia, it has been a pleasure to spend time with you. You gave me a break from... from many things."

He bent over, a quick, one-armed embrace, and deposited a light kiss on the top of her hair.

"Take care of yourself, okay?"

Then he was gone, one arm lifted to get a taxi.

That warm, sexy voice followed her in the press of the subway. It was as if her knees wanted to jump, despite their beating. She felt buoyed as she ran up the stairs to her sister's apartment.

And then she stopped. Tim had been friendly, but no more. And preoccupied by the 'heckling'. To the point he didn't ask for her phone number, nor gave her his.

She felt tears rising behind her eyes. After an effort, she let herself in, ready to play the good aunt for her nephew and nieces. At this hour, her sister was at work and the children still at the playgroup. So she picked her way between toys and notebooks, toward the tiny artificial tree. Her youngest niece's stuffed bunny was already mounting guard. She unloaded her intact boxes, then hid the others in her room.

Later, as she helped prepare a simple spaghetti meal (music was her talent, not cooking), her sis commenting on the stupid jokes her techie co-workers made at her expanse, Felia found a way to retrace Tim.

The radio station.

AFTER DINNER, Felia excused herself from the Monopoly family game, pretexting her exhausting day at the restaurant.

She slipped under her covers, waiting. At the turn of nine, she tuned in the old analog radio, searching for the jazz FM station.

She shivered with joy as she heard a *what a wonderful world,* the deep bass voice of Luis Armstrong. There was another piece, *O Christmas tree,* a slow, almost Zen piano recording by Oscar Peterson. She must have missed the program's opening.

Then as the piano receded, she heard a rich baritone voice, ill-served by the portable radio's sound box.

"In this shortest day of the year, we do believe the light

will return. Before getting to our next piece, I want to share something."

That rich voice belonged to the man she had met.

"Today, I met a special lady… a lady with music in her eyes and her heart. A lady who knew as much about jazz as I do, and that's saying something."

Felia sat up, the city lights streaming through her window's sheer curtains. Was any host supposed to talk about a chance encounter, like that? There was a short pause, and she guessed whisperings inside the studio.

"So, for you, Shakespeare lady, I will have my friend Richard Hamel play a special piece."

Felia was not fooled, he was talking to her, to her only, not mentioning her name. There was another pause, the slight thud of a microphone set down. And the magical piano piece rose. She recognized it instantly: the Zodiac, the Ram part, that Mary Lou Williams dedicated to her musical influences, Billie Holliday and Ben Webster.

She floated in Paradise. Until the end of the broadcast.

"My dear friends, this is my last evening with you. A decision had been taken, to allow this program and its wonderful cast to continue."

An undercurrent of sadness lingered under the rich baritone voice. After a short silence, Tim ended the broadcast with a lighter tone.

"Let's hope that the light will come back, someday."

Then, the musical indicator seeped over, and that was all.

FELIA GOT OFF HER BED. *That can't be true*, she thought.

She padded the floor. Rage suffused her, a red-orange wave flushing up from her feet to her scalp. The situation was clear. The hecklers, Tim had called them. Trolls, her sister would say.

Trolls who have gained a victory. Felia could imagine the river of insults and threats Tim had endured. And if other members of the team had been targeted... She bit her lips. What could she do?

She could hear her sister typing away. Doing more hours, probably unpaid ones.

She stepped out of her room. The kitchen was dark, lit by the greening glow of her sister's laptop. Lucy swiveled on her office chair at her approach. (Her birth name was Lucia, like *Lucia di Lammermoor*, her mother had gushed, too often.)

"Can't sleep, Fel?" she asked.

Lucy had a knack for the computers. She had gone into the same tech college, but the start-up that hired her didn't sink. Now Felia's sister headed one division, despite the grumblings of male underlings. But her wide frame and mean mouth kept the worst offenders away.

"Lucy, I know you've working like a dog, but I need your help..."

Lucy beamed.

"My big musician sister, needing my help? What do you want?"

IT TOOK ONLY five minutes for Lucy to retrieve the info about Timothy Dickson's problems. Five minutes, because there were layers upon layers of dissimulation, and not a river, but a sea of comments, dirty, debasing, even defacing images. She sucked in her breath at a scene showing a torched Toyota.

"This has been going on for almost two years."

"That's why the CBC cancelled the program last year... And nothing was done?"

Lucy sighed like a Disney Princess.

"My dear, of course the CBC did some clean up of the comments, but they were mostly helpless. The budget cuts didn't help. Budget cuts ordered by the same kind of, ahem... 'color-blind' politicians with hordes of social media followers."

"I guess, the kind of followers who claim there are too many women and colored people on the waves..."

The problem had grown branches and branches around Tim. Hecklers hid under sophisticated aliases encrypted with something called TOR, that had nothing to do with the Thor comic book character. The worst had been the torching of his car scant years ago. Lucy's finger pointed to a thread.

"As for the Jazz-FM, they're getting a taste of the same medicine. Look at that *Scktlnts* alias. That's one that appears everywhere. Probably a bot, but I'm not sure. Many interventions under this alias are too precise."

She let out a low whistle.

"Look here: the guy (I am assuming it's a guy, and white) described the exact parking space where Timothy's car was torched."

For a moment, Felia saw again the threatening hood of a Carfati sports car. She leaned over her sister's shoulder and read the letters of the alias. A jolt of anger laced with sadness went through her body.

"Can you tell me when it happened? And where?"

A few taps on the keyboards delivered the answers.

The only thought coming to Felia was: *I know.*

THE NEXT MORNING, Felia put on her sister's Polar Bear hood parka, not taking any chance with the weather. She wasn't a knight in shining armor, but she would do her best, even against an army of trolls.

Armed with a bunch of papers.

The neighborhood had been gentrified, but the red-brick building hadn't changed, just faded a little more since the last time she was there. She walked up the row of metal stairs, made a fist --one right-hand fist-- and knocked on the darkened wood.

She knocked, harder.

At last, steps echoed.

And the door opened, on Zoomer's stunned face.

HE HAD CHANGED, ditching the artsy look and the shades. His eyes were still this clear blue that had drawn her to him. His graying hair was still long, but bound in a tail. He wore his jeans and a long-sleeved blue Tee that hid his arm tattoos, but not the budding belly.

Behind him, she could spy the loft's hardwood floor. The jumble of old CDs, books, partitions, bottles, clothes, pills and food wraps had gone elsewhere. The neat pale wood furniture was Ikea-new. Maybe he had married, but she did not want another woman to go through her path.

"Ophelia, that's you?"

For answer, she brought up her left hand, ungloved. He knew, by a very angry Lucy, that she had broken her piano-playing fingers while flying from him.

"Oh God, I'm so sorry!" he said. "I was an ass. If I could turn back the clock…"

Lame answer, she thought.

Zoomer rubbed his scalp, and that's when she noted the alliance on his left finger. And how he did not smell of tobacco, nor alcohol.

Somehow, he had changed his self-destructing habits, but that didn't mean he was over harassing others. The hecklers' crowd, where her sister sent the list to her security firm intranet (whatever that meant) featured some quite respectable scions of the city.

"We have to talk," she said.

And she presented her second weapon. The sheaf of listings, and transcriptions of his messages.

THE LOFT SMELLED as clean as it looked. The sofa was new. Zoomer had gone for a glass, of juice. At least, her ex was off the drinking. He sipped his orange juice while perusing the list.

"I can't believe it," he said. "I know half the guys on this, I know their alias, I mean. Some were regular fans."

"Really, Zoomer..."

He shook his head.

"I don't go by Zoomer anymore," he said.

She tapped the first alias, a SCKTLNTS with the number 2195, the number of comments registered.

"You didn't think using an alias with the consonants of your group name was a bright idea!"

He protested, almost toppling his glass of juice.

"It wasn't me, I'm telling you! I do not abide by that racist crap. Never did. And, as for the band, we fell apart years ago. You might not believe it, but..."

She had never been that snarky before, but now she felt

an irrepressible urge to yank his leash. Maybe power did corrupt and Felia was a dictator in the making.

Maybe.

"Let me guess: you've changed."

"It's true! Since... well, I kind of ditched the booze. I took time, and therapy, and maybe that's why the band dissolved. I was not as fun as before."

She shifted on the leather sofa, eyeing her notes. The car had been torched, not far from a jazz bar where the group had performed.

"You know I never pressed charges?" she said.

She could have, after the constant yelling.

"And I am grateful, in a way," he said. "Finding this place empty rattled me."

Felia wasn't up to follow any self-pity account.

"So," she said, "you know of most of the guys. And the ringleader, also?"

He nodded, twiddling his gold band.

"I'll help you. But I don't want to get Melody and Yan hurt."

The dictator part inside Felia melted. She had caught the catch in his voice when he pronounced the names. She didn't want anyone (apart from the hecklers) to be hurt, either. Not in this special season of hope.

Fortunately, she had a plan ready.

"Everything will be kept hush-hush. Here's what I need you to do..."

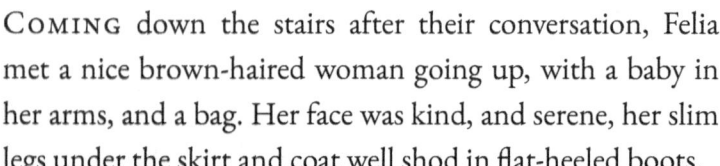

COMING down the stairs after their conversation, Felia met a nice brown-haired woman going up, with a baby in her arms, and a bag. Her face was kind, and serene, her slim legs under the skirt and coat well shod in flat-heeled boots.

"Need a hand?" Felia asked.

The woman smiled.

"No, dear, my husband always helps me up. I guess he must be distracted."

Felia took her leave. Just as she reached the front door, she heard his relieved voice. *Mel! Let me take the tyke!* And the sound of the door closing on the little family.

TWO DAYS LATER, the Jazz FM station announced the return of Timothy Dickson as host for the Christmas week special. At Lucy and Felia's shared apartment, the TV news announced the arrestation of an online harasser, an artist of the jazz scene who resented any other skin color. By interrogating a dozen witnesses identified behind their aliases, they also found the three who torched the car.

"Thanks, sis. You're a pixel angel!"

"You know there isn't a chance in a hundred those charges will stick, don't you?" Lucy asked, drinking hot *chai* tea from her cup.

Felia, ensconced in the chesterfield with a chubby nephew asleep on her lap, shrugged.

"The important thing is, I gave back someone his dream."

She sipped her own cup, filled to the brim with hot cocoa laced with cream. Oh, she just wished she could see Tim's bright smile again!

ON THE 24TH OF DECEMBER, a day of mad errands, her phone rang when she was stacking pastries in Lucy's green refrigerator. She didn't recognize the number. Was it one uncaptured heckler? She clicked the answer button.

"Er, hello?"

The warm and furry voice at the other end melted her inside.

"Felia? It's me."

A chair magically materialized under her, pushed by her sister.

"T-Tim? How did you find me? I thought..."

A chuckle, like little fingers tickling her insides.

"Something wonderful happened in the last days," he said. "And, according to my sources, your name came up as my good fairy."

"Your sources?"

"Let's say the police, the security firm and you did a

fine work. My online hecklers and their fraudulent accounts vanished overnight. Brigit is also relieved."

Felia jumped to her feet.

"Lucy! Did you…"

Lucy, busy playing with her youngest daughter and her stuffed bunny, rose her brows in mock innocence.

"So, before my Christmas Eve broadcast tonight, I would like to get acquainted with you again. The real you."

He explained his plans. She gasped aloud.

"The Ritz? It's too expensive…"

"I'm sending a taxi at your place at four. Put on your best dress."

She tried a last-ditch effort at economy. She knew how dire his financial situation was.

"No fast-food counter for you, my dear battling angel."

"But, why?"

"Because," he said, "you are worth splurging a bit."

THE TAXI DRIVER REFUSED PAYMENT, telling her fare had already been covered. Felia blubbered something as the same man held the door.

That's when she discovered a glassed-in lobby, not a restaurant. A dark-haired woman in a pair of tight jeans, crystalline eardrops, and a V-neck ugly Christmas sweater beckoned.

"Ms. Felia, I'm happy to meet you! I'm Carla. I work with Tim."

She helped Felia out of her coat and hung it on a rack.

"Oh my god. You are ravishing!"

Felia, all decked out in low pumps and a calf-reaching scarlet gown, wearing her mother's pearl necklace, blushed. She had at least ten years over this eager young thing but it felt nice to receive a sincere compliment.

"Tim told us a lot about what you did to help us."

Felia shrugged. It hadn't sounded like a lot, from her point of view. A few phone calls from her computer-savvy sister to her colleagues. A visit to her ex. The police did the rest.

She followed the talkative young woman through security, up a lift to a nice, carpeted lobby, focusing on the funny jingle bells-wearing reindeers on the back of the sweater. The woman, Carla, was a news anchor, despite her young age. Felia was duly impressed, and told her so.

"The big cannons are all vacationing so the rest of us pitch in, you know."

Carla pushed a glassy door, and gestured for Felia to enter.

"Here you are, Ms. Felia. Now, I've got to prepare for my five-o-clock news!"

Then she was gone, the reindeers running amok on her back as she scissored away.

Felia felt out of her depth. She searched for a familiar

face in the tumble of sound technicians and scripts and assistants.

"Ah, Felia, you're just in time!"

His voice enveloped her as she turned. There he stood, legs camped, clad in a fitting tuxedo with a white waistband, as if he was about to host the Screen Awards Ceremony. His bountiful hair looked ready to explode off the red string that bound them.

He presented Brigid, a silver-haired TV journalist turned radio host who gratefully pumped her hand. Then his team, among them Richard Hamel, a redhaired pianist with an infectious smile. She remembered his deft interpretation of her favorite pieces.

Tim took her arm, as if she was a delicate plant, and leaned close.

"Before we go, I want to show you something else."

He guided her through a soundproof slab lined with cork and noise absorbers. Inside the smaller room, she was greeted by a vision from paradise.

A dark, shiny grand piano filled the studio, smiling with all its black and white keys.

A CLEAN HIGH-CARBON steel smell rose from the wires, kept in check by the harmonic table. The air was dry, the moisture pushed away somehow. She had the impression that blowing on those strings would make them sing.

"Our guests play on this Yamaha, and it is recorded."

He showed her the hanging microphone in its dark bubble of moss. His hand pushed, again gently, on the small of her back.

"Try it. Please."

Felia advanced, her flat pumps pit-patting the hardwood to the black beast. There, she sat on the bench, adjusting her gown. She felt like a little girl again, playing Mozart at school, making her grandma proud.

She placed her hands on the ivory keys.

The first note, a no-nonsense, basic C, sounded like the warm embrace of her grandma after her school concert. Then she hit a low B minor, the darkness seeping in as her studies receded and her debts mounted. As her string of bad relationships crossed her mind, her crooked fingers hammered the keys in a discordant cacophony.

She stopped, raising her hands, ashamed of wounding such a majestic instrument. She was not Mary Lou.

"I, I can't," she said in a whisper, as the echo of the disharmonious chords died off.

However, Tim prodded her forward. His warm hand settled on her shoulder, like a soft-feathered bird. He sat on the corner of the bench, not crowding her.

"I'm not a pianist at all, Felia. But *you* are."

That most harmonious, stable male voice box echoed inside her, a resonance running deep, a golden light reaching into her darkest recesses.

"Even if no one ever recognize your value," Tim said, his voice rumbling.

He was leaning so close he could kiss her, if she wished. (And she knew with absolute certainty that Tim would never do anything without her consent).

"I will sing it under every roof, under the stars."

Hope, light green as spring leaves, filled her like water in the desert. And, with her eyes wide open, she drew closer and kissed him. She felt his full lips respond, their breaths mingle from lung to lung to lung. His arms enfolded her, his beard tickling her cheek. He smelled of wood and soap and faint mint, of snow and water, of loyalty and confidence...

She was a happy Ophelia drowning in a lake of bliss.

When they parted, for breath, Tim spoke, his eyes lit up by more than the projectors.

"Please, my dear lady knight, please, play your soul out and fill my heart."

Her fingers forgot about the old fracture and twisted phalanxes as Felia managed to play a rendition of Dave Brubeck's *Santa is coming to Town*, the tempo slow enough to let her gain confidence.

Then she embarked on a jazz cover of *I'll be Home for Christmas*, a piece she had played so long ago at school, then one piano arrangement of *Merry Christmas to You*, originally sung by Nat King Cole, before daring to interpret the Zodiac suite composed by Williams.

She didn't stop there, even if her stomach growled.

Playing became easier, it felt like easing into a warm water pool under the stars. She lost herself in the magic until, glancing sideways, she met Tim's roguish smile.

The glass partition separating them from the studio had filled with the crew, all looking at her with rapt eyes. Were they recording her?

Felia didn't mind. Now, her fairy-like fingers, fully awaken from their long dormancy, gave life to more complex jazz and blues. And, just maybe, they slipped in a melody genuinely radiating from her soul.

As she played, sitting by the man who loved her, Felia felt the comforting presence of Mary Lou Williams, a gentle ghost watching from the dark blue sky.

HER STAR OF GLADNESS

IN THE AIR over the Pacific Ocean

MADELYN COOKE DID her best to ignore the unending growl of the engines and the revelers singing out of tune two rows behind her. Alas, the thick smell coming from the skin pores exuding alcohol found its way to her nose. One more *Santa Came to Toooown*, and she would ask for a change of seats. There were some empty spaces at the rear.

She twisted on her seat to look at the night behind the triple-layered window. The country lay in total darkness, no city lights dotting the dark expanse under the wing. She suddenly felt cold, as if the high altitude air had found its way inside the pressurized cabin. Maybe she should have splurged for a seat in the first-class section, but her savings went only so far. She had chosen the night flight, the cheapest, only one stopover, then landing at Honolulu in the morning.

The loud singing eventually abated, under the firm steward's voice, a guy with a linebacker's shoulders. The seat's fabric, a dull gray-blue in the toned-down cabin light, reminded her of the second-hand couch in her apartment. She had stowed her winter coat in the overhead compartment, grateful for her optimal combination of travel clothes, accessories and knick-knacks that held in the small shoulder bag under the next seat.

She had looked upon the circus of rigid cabin suitcases that angry passengers jostled in the tiny storage spaces. Why, all those incompressible hard shells were the fashion, now? It had been a while since last she took a plane to go somewhere.

At last, the pandemic that had kept her cooped up three whole years in her Manhattan flat (that she kept because the rent had been frozen) had receded in the rear mirror. Few wore face covers, except to avoid catching a cold. Madelyn had taken a great pleasure in planning her holiday escape, something her husband would never have tolerated until he did his own escape, starting a new life and (she sighed) a new family. Flaunting his last born on her email had been a low blow.

Madelyn lived alone; all her friends and sisters celebrated Christmas in the warmth of their own families, in different cities.

She had left the flat undecorated, no tree, no tinsels.

For once, she would not pass another miserable holiday period, alone with the Hallmark canal and take-out food, or alone in those parties arranged for older bachelors. Not her style.

Madelyn was eager to leave the cold and the slush behind her. She closed her eyes, envisioning the warm evenings walking on the beach, listening to waves instead of the traffic under her flat's windows, and maybe, just maybe...

A shiver run up her spine.

Madelyn had fled, leaving a daughter behind. A distraught daughter who had shown up at her door two days ago.

Emily, she thought, *have I done the right thing?*

Oh, her dear Emily had assured her she would manage in her absence. Her grown-up daughter had settled in her old room, but her spirits had taken a dive. Yes, she had lost her job and would be looking for a new one. But would she manage her medications? Madelyn should have insisted that her daughter board the flight with her. There was certainly room enough on the plane.

Her angular face suddenly flared in the window, courtesy of the overhead light switch. The wrong switch.

"Oops, sorry," her seat neighbor said.

An arm rose, flicking the switches.

In the press and stress of boarding, nagged by the thought of her daughter going back home alone (and did Emily take a taxi, the sensible solution?) she had not been aware of her surroundings. The B seat next to her A seat was filled by a solid man in a red cotton sweatshirt, his dark eyes twinkling over a strong nose and wide cheekbones. The thick paperback he had opened the overhead light for rested on his knees, opened. That one must be in the thousand pages range.

"Is it good?" Madelyn asked.

Her voice sounded to her ears like a long-time smoker's, which she wasn't. The cabin air, too dry, irritated her throat. The way his eyes crinkled around his contrite smile told her the man was about her own age bracket, even if the thick mane bound in a ponytail was a rich brown. Madelyn's hair had turned silver in the years after the divorce, and she didn't see the relevance of hiding their color.

"Hu-uh," he said. "I'm almost finished, so if you like historical novels, you can have it."

"Oh, but you don't have to," she said.

He rose the book, the telltale fuzzy gray of the read pages stopping at the two-thirds.

"I'll be finished before we land. And a good book is to share."

When he plunged back into his doorstopper, abstaining from commenting on either plot or characters, she knew he was a true reader. She felt a huge bubble of approval mounting in her, which was unusual since she didn't know this man. She fingered the bright tourism brochures peeking from the back seat pocket. She felt an aura of calm radiating from his bent head. Eventually the weariness won and she settled for a few hours of sleep.

Daniel K Inouye International Airport (Honolulu)

MADELYN HAD THOUGHT she had been well-prepared for Hawaii. She had read a lot about the volcanic archipelago, even started the celebrated James Michener book, but the long introduction lost her. She had envisioned hiking on the flanks of the Mauna Loa volcano, and exploring paths in dreamy forests or sandy beaches, whichever came first.

She had chosen Hawaii because her passport was outdated, and this was a warm place she could go that was still in the same country.

Now, carried in the throng of deplaned passengers, she felt like a straw floating in a rushing river, with a weird mix of Hawaiian Aloha and Christmas jingles raining from the sound system. Had she done a good thing? The question bounced along with her fellow passengers trailing giant rolling suitcases and golf bags. She had put sensible shoes, at least, but her shoulder bag weighted more with the thick paperback wedged inside. She had seen it was a fictional account of the Darwin's voyage onboard the Beagle.

She had left her nice seat neighbor at the luggage port,

and proceeded to the exit. She had expected to walk miles and miles in corridors packed with store fronts and peppered with Holiday trinkets and cheering Santas, drenched with canned Christmas music. Instead, minutes from exiting the plane, she was outside meeting the heat, the light and a fierce blue sky.

A sea of taxis and cars waited, fellow tourists in bright T-shirts and hats milling around. Farther, stood the Honolulu skyscrapers she had only seen on TV as a child watching *Hawaii 5-0*. She had pictured flower necklaces thrown over her, but the only ones she saw were on sale in a florist's boutique.

The sun had crept up, sending reflection in her eyes. She turned back after a few steps: the Honolulu airport looked like a five-story lump of brown sugar dropped on the runways.

She suddenly felt terribly tired as she raised an arm to call a taxi. None came.

Modernity had hit while she wasn't looking: most travelers had called from their phone app. She pulled up her own credit-card-sized phone from her pants' pocket and flipped it open. The screen returned an empty battery signal. She thought she had shut it off, but she must have forgotten. In the long hours of flight, the battery had drained itself dry, questing in vain for a WiFi signal.

Beside all the stress of landing in a strange place on the shortest day of the year, worry for her daughter peaked. She couldn't call to tell Emily she had made it safely. Too absorbed in her problem, she gasped when a shadow cut the sun.

"Do you need help?"

Her plane neighbor carried a cabin sports bag under one arm and trailed a suitcase that could have contained two entire wardrobes. The man stood close enough for her to appreciate the absence of either tobacco or alcohol on his breath, something unexpected, considering all the complimentary drinks offered aboard.

He had dispensed with the sweatshirt and wore a powder-blue shirt over his barrel chest, chino pants and running shoes. In the light of day rising over Oahu, he looked fabulous, the golden-brown skin of his forearms populated with pliant hair, like a prairie. He wore no hat on his mane, only a pair of reflecting shades, her startled face looking back at her in each.

Madelyn, having survived the Enron debacle that had siphoned off her savings and (later) her husband, had never been at a loss for words. Her eloquence had allowed her to keep her modest 114th street apartment, where a bylaw prevented evictions and exaggerated rent hikes. But now, she was groping for something nice and proper to say.

"I, er, yes, I think so," she said, her throat dry.

"Are you staying here for long?" he asked, expertly tapping on his passport-sized cell.

Again, that simple question wove its sluggish way through a forest of awkward neurons.

"Um, three weeks," she said, looking at the giant brown

sugar lump rising behind her, also reflected in his glasses. "It's my first time, here."

She would have stayed a month or two if she could afford it. Then she stomped on this thought. Her daughter might need her, or the building's renters association might have to deal with another sly attempt to evict them.

His smile gobbled half his face under the shades, straining lines like theater curtains.

"Good," he said. "Long enough to start appreciating the islands."

Still hazy in her head (she *should* have eaten the complimentary biscuits before leaving the plane), she recalled that there were six main islands and a dozen smaller outcrops and natural preserves in the archipelago. Oahu, where she stood, was the most populated. The largest island, called Hawaii like the state, home of the biggest volcano…

She became intensely aware of his presence, and a question popped in her mind, a social nicety she should have returned sooner.

"And you, are you visiting, or returning home?"

"Both," he said.

He waved a wide hand at the voluminous suitcase.

"I'm visiting my daughters," he said.

Madelyn hadn't noticed any band on his annular, but those days, men often forgot them. Of course, he had a family! Something clicked inside her, like it had all the times her path had crossed interesting, but unavailable men. *Do not cross*. She had always prided herself on being proper, on never preying on other men.

Except that this time, that *Do not cross* warning hit like a door closing on her fingers.

A soft, single *oh* escaped her lips before she could stop it.

In novels, that would be the moment when a cloud passed in front of the sun, changing the mood. But the tropical sky ignored her resolution and stayed resolutely clear. She opened her mouth to say the proper thing, again, *how nice*, or *good for you*.

He let out a short bark of laughter.

"Oh, my, you have *jet lag* written all over your face," he said. "Let's share a taxi, to get you to your hotel. If it's your first time, they would have put you at the Hyatt Regency, or the Hilton."

Despite her resolve, she smiled at his wit. The agent had booked her at the Hilton.

"You're right, I'm at the Hilton. But after, I'm not sure where I'll stay. I had reserved an excursion ticket on the volcano park," she said, "and after that, the botanical garden... I read about the biodiversity of Hawaii, with plants and birds living only here."

His face lit up, shedding years from his age.

"If you like walking, there are several botanical gardens on the archipelago," he said. "The best known is the Tropical Botanical Garden."

"Is it a walking distance from here?"

Another short bark that seemed to come from the depts of his capacious thoracic cage.

"You would have to swim there!" he said. "That garden is on the Big Island."

She remembered that Big Island was the name of the biggest Island, also called Hawaii, to avoid confusion. A canary-yellow car slowed down. The man opened the door for Madelyn, before jostling the huge suitcase in the trunk. When he settled his bulk next to her on the false leather back seat, she became once more intensely aware of his presence.

"I appreciate your traveling light," he said. "I'm always lugging tons of material."

"I don't want to impose on you," she said. "If it is out of your way, I can pay my share."

Madelyn was aware of her babbling like a teenager, but she was sternly decided to do the proper thing. She would recharge her phone at the hotel, talk to her daughter, and plan her next steps.

"I rent a flat at Manoa, close to Honolulu University."

In her hazy state, it took her several seconds to process that *flat* and *family man* were two separate notions.

"The University? If I may be so bold, what is your occupation, mister, er...?" she asked.

"Dr. Makoa Kalama. I teach undergraduate botany. I'm back from a congress in New York."

Botany? No wonder he was so acquainted with the natural parks!

"Madelyn Cooke. I was an accountant, once upon a time. But I retired."

He eyed her appreciatively.

"Retired, but quite active, if you plan to hike the Hawaii National Volcano Park."

She nodded, pleased with herself. It felt good to bask in the glow of his comfortable presence. *His wife must be so lucky*, she thought.

The taxi mingled in the Honolulu circulation, dense, but a far cry from the New York honking circus. There was so much to see! She absorbed herself in the architecture of the buildings streaming by, until the taxi turned on Kalia road, and she got a glimpse of a nice rainbow on the side of a thin building and, just as close, the blue-green expanse of the Pacific.

The taxi stopped at the entrance of the Hilton Hawaiian Village Waikiki Beach Resort.

Already, she thought. She grabbed her shoulder bag, her other hand advancing to the handle. But Kalama got out of the cab and was already pulling her door open. A real gentleman. Madelyn took her time to loop the strap of her pack over her head.

"We-ell, it has been a pleasure, doctor Kalama" she said, finding her proper stance, extending her hand.

Neat and proper. He took her hand in a firm but gentle handshake. Not compressing her fingers like some too-assertive men did.

"It has been a pleasure, too, Mrs. Cooke."

He lifted his shades, revealing his dark chocolate irises lit up by the sun's glare. His brows were as brown as his hair, but a few white threads. His smile warmed her all over.

"I hope you like your stay here," he said.

Suddenly, he fished out a wrinkled card from his pants, with a green university of Hawaii circle. "If you ever need some pointers on where to go on your visit, you can call me."

She felt horribly tired, but elated as she accepted the card. "I would very much like that," she said.

Madelyn waited until the yellow spot was lost in the circulation, one hand gripping the strap of her shoulder bag. Dr Kalama would make a good friend.

A few minutes later, Madelyn found herself in the cleanest, most peaceful room she had ever been in, all done in whites and dove grays, the sheets smelling of baby powder, with a balcony overlooking the Pacific. She was high enough to see a bit of the famous Pearl Harbor, a trident of water plunged in the flank of Oahu Island.

The silence, with only the sea and the shore birds cackling their wishes, was restful. She bent over the side table to plug her cellphone to the wall outlet, feeling drained of energy herself. She barely had time to discard her clothes and flop down on the cloud-soft bed before losing herself in sleep.

∾

WHEN SHE OPENED one eye (the other was pressed against the pillow), the flat clock by the bed told her the afternoon was well-advanced. She had overslept, too late now to go on an excursion. She swiveled her feet off the bed with ease, not a muscle protesting. At least, she felt rested. And hungry.

Madelyn reveled in the shower and the hibiscus-perfumed soap. She felt all the weariness of winter drain from her along with the water.

She came off the shower, not looking at her reflection in the mirror as she toweled herself. She tried to assess her body and hair and face as a man would, but shut the exercise. Pointless. The nice professor had a family, she would not betray them. She dried her hair with the towel, grateful for the mild December temperatures in Hawaii. Then, still wrapped in the terrycloth towel, she took out the brochures and spread them on the double bed, studying the possibilities.

She couldn't tell how long she had been poring over the maps, when she heard a buzzing and found her cell dancing on the side table. By Jove, she had forgotten to call Emily! Now, her daughter was calling to make sure she had arrived.

"Hi Mom! I'm so happy you got there!"

Madelyn's guilt rose. She recalled Emily's disheveled hair when she had stumbled at her door, reeling from a job loss. And of an obvious heartache.

"Are you well? Is it going okay for a new job? The landlord didn't gave you trouble?"

A bubbly laugh sounded from her daughter's end. The street noises told her Emily was currently walking in the city. An ambulance siren, receding. Engines strumming. A taxi klaxon, aggressively honking. A dog barking in the background.

"Nah, I'm A-Okay. Well, even more than OK. *(A bubbly whisper.)* Well, that's it, Mom. Say hello to the sea for me!"

After they disconnected, Madelyn rewound the conversation in her mind. Emily's voice had a lilt any mother would recognize. And that hurried whispering. Uh-oh. Her daughter had met someone.

And whether that someone was good or bad news for Em, she couldn't do anything about it.

MADELYN WAS STILL DECIDING if she would eat at the hotel restaurant, or try one of the brochure's suggestions, like in a moored boat, when the room's phone rang. She had given her room's number to Em, hadn't she?

"Yes, Emily?" she blurted.

The voice on the other side sounded amused.

"I do not know this Emily, but I sure envy her."

"Oh, doctor Kalama! Emily's my daughter."

Silly her! The doctor must have called the hotel and asked for her name.

"She didn't come with you?" he asked.

A flurry of guilt passed through her. This was Christmas time, and Emily would be so alone.

"She is... looking for a new job," she said.

"Well. I was wondering, since I'm only going to visit my daughters for Christmas Eve, if I could show you around. There's a restaurant I think that you would love."

She had decided not to get attached, but she ached for company. She stammered.

"Yes, er, that would be lovely. Where are you?"

"In the lobby."

It seemed to Madelyn that she had lost forty years as she giggled like a teen, trying on her outfits. Fortunately, she had no more than three, tops and lower parts interchangeable.

She decided on a floral print chiffon dress, white with red and purple flowers, and a pair of low-heeled slip-on shoes that could be flattened to fit in a small bag. The fabric was light, stretchy and utterly compressible, the sleeves long enough to hide her sun-spotted shoulders. She added a light cardigan in a matching hue, in case the evening got chilly.

She swallowed her saliva in the lift going down. The

mirror panels reflected her silhouette and silver hair done up in her customary bun. She was free, for a rare time in her life. And passing a few hours with a friendly man would give a nice start to her vacation.

When she got off the elevator, Doctor Kalama unfolded his frame from the couch, clad in a flamboyant aloha orange shirt printed with palms, over a pair of off-white jeans. He had a nice balanced body and wide shoulders, and his hair were combed and pulled tight into a ponytail.

Without the shades, she could see the glimmer in his eyes when she sashayed her way to him, the printed dress flowing around her calves.

"I hope you know a place," she said, "because I am famished."

He offered his elbow, and she took it. They walked out of the hotel, and immediately, like a dream, the soft sand of the beach. How long had it been since she walked so carefree, at the arm of a man?

The beach extended as far as Madelyn could see, with the rising crater in view. She had expected the place to be filled with reclining bodies, but the cooler evening air had chased most of the tourists to the inside venues. Coming from the New York January weather, she barely felt it.

"You are quite elegant," she said.

He extended his arms sideways.

"Because I fear I might not get another chance to enjoy your company," he said, his generous lips stretching into a mischievous smile. "So here I am, all decked out like a courting I'iwi bird."

Madelyn was divided between giggling like a schoolgirl or scolding the man. My, but he *was* going lengths to woo her!

Time to bring some reality in.

"I hope your wife doesn't mind," she said in a so-natural, so-reasonable tone.

She tensed for his response.

Married men could exhibit weird reactions when rebuffed. She hoped he would not stomp away. But he threw his head backward and barked this warm laugh.

"Oh-oh! Afraid my dear Halia will swoop on you, all claws out?"

He made a scene of peering like an eagle at the horizon, reminding her of a Hanna-Barbera cartoon character.

"Hmm, not seeing her around. Just the gulls."

Madelyn felt her cheek grow hot from embarrassment. Was he mocking his wife? And, worst, was *she* encouraging him like a cheerleader? She sank the points of her shoes in the sand, crossed her arms over her throbbing heart as if to silence it and raised her chin.

Then she summoned the stern, serious, *don't mess with me mister* voice she had used with a couple of slick adventurers she had dated not so long ago.

"Doctor Kalama, if you're married, I don't think it would be proper to dine out."

He stopped his pantomime, his eyes rounded in dismay.

"If your students happen to see you with another woman..."

Madelyn Cooke would never, *e-ver* dabble in three-sided relations. She had been on the losing side once, and she would not inflict this soul-crushing pain on another woman.

Kalama blinked, then spurt a Santa-like "Hohoho!" bark, and re-enacted the pantomime of looking around, his thick brows knotted.

Dang, but he was charming, in his goofy way! If he was like the slick guys she had dated before (*before* meaning: before they got wise about the real state of her finances and fled), at least Kalama was entertaining.

He stretched one arm toward the harbor, where a pair of triangular sails looking like quotation marks pointed at the sky. He had two deep scars, like a cat's clawing, on the back of his hand.

"Mrs. Cooke, I think we're both hungry. If we are to discuss my family, it's better to get a table between us!" he said.

This time, Madelyn was certain her face had gone as red as the I'ivi bird that was the emblem of Hawaii.

THEY TOOK a yellow cab to get to a place on Pier 38, to a place called Marco's Fish Market that didn't look at all like a fish market.

Her stomach growling, she followed him inside a nice little restaurant, stopping to gape at the huge swordfish hanging on the entrance wall, its sword pointed at the register, like a direction.

Their table was close to a wall of floor-to-ceiling windows, with smart shades pulled down to stop the direct sun. At first, the plain chairs made her afraid of being uncomfortable, but her back rested easily on the curved dossier.

Madelyn fingered the menu, deciphering the meals' names, and the small pictures. She did not want to upset her stomach with grilled seafood, so she settled for a plain meal, a plate of braised mushrooms looking like round pebbles, with an egg thrusted over them and rich yellow maize bread on the side. She took her time, because she was still unsure about what to do.

Her first day in Hawaii, and already a man hitting on her? Maybe it was too pat.

She observed him as he studied the menu. He looked in his late fifties or early sixties, older than the men who had dated her since the divorce, all of them struggling 'between relations'. (Eligible men in Madelyn's age bracket tended to chase much younger women.)

Oblivious to her scrutiny, Kalama folded his menu with a gentle clap. A serene-looking lady in her fifties took their orders, his Misoyaki Chilean sea bass and her braised mushrooms.

They sipped water, waiting for their meals and, in Madelyn's case, wondering about plunging too fast into a new relation. She was conscious of his gaze passing like a gull over her head, never lingering. She focused on the harbor behind the large windows. They were closer to the bizarre quotation mark sails. They were attached to a double hull that looked like two giant canoes bound together. The strange sail boat looked made of pale, golden wood.

"What is this boat? I never saw one like this."

"This is the *Hōkūleʻa*," he said.

"Hokulea? Hoku means star, does it?"

His smile rewarded her.

"Its name means *Star of Gladness*. This ship was built in 1976, entirely using Polynesian traditional techniques. And they did a first trip, using the traditional navigation."

"Oh, like the Kon-Tiki," she said.

"Yes. The builders wanted to revive the legacy of exploration and ingenuity that brought the first Polynesians to the archipelago of Hawaiʻi. You are quite lucky today, because the Star of Gladness is often sailing around the world. Here is where the ship comes to dock."

Madelyn felt many little stars blooming in her stomach.

Kalama went on to talk about the boat, about his students' projects, and his daughters living on Maui Island. She dwelled lightly on her former life, brushing over the

Enron debacle and the divorce. Only when she mentioned Emily did her throat catch.

But at this moment, the graceful waitress deposited colorful plates in front of them. Madelyn was ravenous, after their walk on the beach and devoured the pebble-shaped mushrooms in cheese sauce. They were at an early hour, with few diners. She enjoyed the companiable silence, while letting the ambient sounds pass through her. No holiday music background marred the peace.

The braised mushrooms settled down without waging battle in her digestive system, and that in itself was a victory. No anti-acid required.

She finished an exquisite poached pear with vanilla gelato dessert, that sated her belly. How long had it been since she ate so well? When the graceful waitress presented the note, the doctor's hand caught the paper, like a fish.

"Oh, I can pay," she said, fingers blundering in her purse for her VISA.

But he had already proffered his phone, and the invisible exchange clicked on.

"Do not think of it, Mrs. Cooke."

It was chivalrous of him, but that put her in a debtor position. Which brought her concerns crashing like a wave. She needed to know.

"So," she said in a light tone, "am I dating a married man?"

"Ah," he raised the napkin in mock defense. "The big moral question."

Again, this amused tone.

"Kalia and I married young, students in the throes of a devouring passion," he said, his voice low. "It took a few years and two babies to find out that we were not compatible, and more years still to divorce, because we wanted to make sure our girls were well set in life before splitting. Our parents were disappointed, of course."

Madelyn felt grateful for his candor. Her relieved expression did not go unnoticed. His fingers brushed lightly over hers.

"So no, I did not abandon Kalia. My ex-wife's happy as a lark, doing computer research on the mainland with her husband. We speak to each other from time to time, like old friends."

That was certainly not Madelyn's marital experience. She had been left alone to see to Emily...

WHEN THEY EXITED THE RESTAURANT, they walked around the quay toward the *Hōkūleʻa* and its quotation marks sails. She was treated to a view of the sixty-foot long voyaging canoe, with too many riggings to keep count. The simple shelter was balanced on a platform between the two hulls, with the galleys over the hulls. Since the first voyage, more modern navigational instruments had been fitted to the craft, for safety.

She noticed the solid, hand-weaved nets everywhere.

She imagined the hardy sailors leaving their island, with no life jackets, nothing to protect them except their wits. She let the young guide, obviously a student, explain how the ancestral sailors used the star Arcturus to guide them.

The sails were imprinted with a bird silhouette, with a sharp two-pronged tail. She had seen those before.

"Are they frigatebirds?" she asked.

"The biggest bird on the island, yes. The *iwa* bird always knows where he is going. The sailors tried to imitate him."

A wide wooden beam was engraved with the words *Kapu nā Keiki*.

"This is the motto of the ship."

"What does it mean?"

"*Hold sacred the children*," Kalama translated.

Protecting the children. Madelyn's heart constricted, and she grabbed the beam.

"Are you unwell?" Kalama asked, holding her shoulder bag aloft.

She took a ragged breath, as if she had run ten kilometers, and filled her eyes with the azure, pierces by the masts, where gulls soaring over it, their graceful wings lulling the humans to forget they were here for the food, first.

"Yes I am," she lied.

She had been thinking of one child, in particular...

LATER, they took a cab to a park at the foot of the big crater called the Diamond Head. They walked through short, dry grass, past an outdoor theater that promised a rich cultural life. She looked up at the vast riddled slope rising from a band of dark green trees, the rock painted in pink overtones by the setting sun.

"Was it a meteor strike?" she asked.

"The Diamond Head is the remnant of a volcano," he said, stomping his foot on the dark ground. "We are walking on the ejecta, and that gives a rich soil."

They walked under a thicket of trees, a mix of pines and weeping willows. The drooping branches brushed by her carefully done bun. As she stopped to pull her hair in shape, she heard an eerie whisper when the wind passed through the pines. Looking at her feet, she saw the fallen ten-inch-long needles, each with a stubby end.

"What are those trees?"

"Ah. *Casuarina equisetum*. The whispering pines, even if they're not technically, conifers."

His foot pushed around the litter of long needles.

"But like conifers, Casuarina's leaves hinder the germination of understory plants."

"Because it is too acid," Madelyn said.

His delighted smile warmed her.

"Exactly! You wouldn't think this tree belongs to the same class as the flowering plants, but it does. This is why Hawaii is such a fantastic place. Nine out of ten things growing here don't grow anywhere else in the world."

She could feel the passion in his voice as they walked amicably. And, contrary to the slick guys, she felt safe in his company.

An outcrop of rock stood in their way, a volcanic boulder apparently forgotten there by a distracted god.

Kalama extended his wide, scarred hand. She took it, and he pulled her up without a hitch. She hadn't expected him to be this strong, still. Many men in their age bracket had to contend with various illnesses.

Soon, they stood on the flat, grainy volcanic rock. The actual Diamond crown was towering over them, but here they could look over the busy Honolulu downtown, and out to the sea fleeing to the western horizon, where arrow-tailed frigatebirds darted here and there, diving into the clear waters. The *iwa* bird, Madelyn had read, always knew its way back.

She pulled up her cardigan. He drew closer.

"May I?" he asked, ever the gentleman.

In a move as slow as the Mauna Loa lava flow, to leave her time to step back if she objected, he draped his arm over her shoulders, a warm scarf. He didn't lean his weight on her, and she felt he was supporting her in a way. Her own hand crept up, feeling the hardened tissue of the scars near the knuckles.

"What happened to your hand?" she asked.

"Nothing heroic. I slipped and fell over some cactus while collecting samples. Par for the course of being a botanist."

They stayed, unmoving, until the red ball of the sun sank in a drapery of clouds, and after the last ray, the clouds repeated the fantastic colors. Madelyn knew that many painters would find happiness in here.

She didn't feel time pass, the sea breeze blowing her hair, the scents of the cotton shirt and skin, the moans of the whispering pines, the low, clock-regularity of the waves lapping at the beach, so far below. The Gauguin-like colors painted the sky a dark red, turning into a indigo blue. She had missed this special twilight hue, living in the big city.

That day had been the best of her life, filling her with wonders. She couldn't believe she had found this incredible man.

"This has been an unexpected, wonderful day," she said.

And to say I barely talked to you in the plane!

His voice, low and rumbling, the vibration spreading in her ear pressed against his chest.

"This day has been good for me, too," he said.

She let out an amused whimper.

"I can't believe you did not go out in all those years."

A rumble, like a slow seism.

"Do I look like a bad boy?"

"Well, er... "

"Exactly. And not even when I was younger. Kalama means *torch*, but I assure you there's nothing fiery in me. I was immersed in my research, my books, the congresses. Nothing exciting there, move along, young Jedi."

She snorted at the Star Wars quip.

"I have had enough of the 'exciting' kind of guys, doctor."

"Madelyn, --can I call you Madelyn?" he asked. "And yes, you can call me Makoa," he added in such a hurry his syllables collided like wobbling pins in a bowling alley.

She nodded. He took her hands in a butterfly-gentle grip.

"So, Madelyn. I know it is a bit soon, but I would be happy to invite you for Christmas Eve in Maui, in my family's house."

"That's where your daughters live?"

"Yes. House market has gone as mad here as anywhere else, so that house will stay in the family."

Twin little stars shone in his dark eyes under the curves of his eyebrows. A soft tingling rose in her spine, a tingling that told her he -- Makoa -- was sincere, and elated to have her celebrating Christmas in his family. And she felt a joyful response bubbling inside her...

She heard in her mind another bubbly voice.

Emily. Alone. Or in bad company. She had had a hunch her daughter's latest boyfriend had rather been a boy*fiend*.

She had tried to call Emily from the restaurant's bathrooms, getting an a *out of service* signal. She pictured herself, feasting and laughing, while...

"Doctor, er, Makoa," she said, tasting those intimate syllables on her tongue. "I am honored by your invitation, really, I'm touched that you can open your home to a stranger..."

Her eloquence dropped like the whispering pines' branches. While she reached for new words to mend the cut sentence, her new friend's voice inserted itself.

"There is a *but* hidden in your words, isn't it?" he asked.

She felt the tears rising to her eyes. How *could* she feast and rejoice with this man and his family, when her own daughter was alone in the flat, depressed, or tangled in another horrendous relationship? What if Emily had forgotten to take her medications?

Madelyn blinked, not wanting to inflict her pain on this fine man.

"I, I can't intrude on your family celebration," she said, her words as unsteady as canoes in a storm.

"You're not intruding, you would be my guest. Otherwise, well, you will be alone on Christmas."

It wouldn't be the first time, she wanted to say. But she didn't want to hurt him.

"I just can't. They don't know me."

She had kept her body rigid as she spoke, in control. But she felt a fat tear oozing from the inside corner of her left eye. Before she could raise her hand to brush it off, it rolling down her cheek, her chin, then off.

He moved, then, so fast. He raised his index, the drop shining like a tiny diamond.

"Waimaka o na hoku," he said, in a soft voice. "It means, 'tear of a star'. A most delicate offering."

She swallowed her saliva.

"N-not like the star of gladness," she blurted.

He looked at the round liquid pearl on his finger. She wondered if he would lick the tear like in old sappy movies.

"But as precious," he said. "Only close friends share tears."

He reverently let the tear fall from the tip of his index to the forest floor.

"The island received your gift, Madelyn," he said.

The poetic shook her sense of proper, but she held fast to the idea of Emily. Over them, the trees' flowing branches chattered with the wind in vegetal gossip.

"I, I might have to go back home," she said. "And..."

Her throat closed. More tears flowed, a river of them, more gifts to the dry volcanic soil. She imagined plants sprouting from the soil. She felt old, old and powerless...

His arms went around her in a fluid gesture, as if he had read her mind. Not crushing her, just holding her as wracking sobs tore her, a frail boat moored in a safe harbor.

How he took her back from the Diamond Head to the Hilton Madelyn did not remember. Could have been a taxi or a flying carpet. But here they were, like by magic, standing at the doors of the thin rainbow-colored building.

Madelyn was aware of the swish of waves licking the sand, of the noises of revelers on the beach, the good skin-and-sweat smell of the man looking down at her, with those unfathomable eyes and flaring laugh lines.

"I, I guess this is good bye," she said.

She expected him to answer with a trite *you have my number* line, but instead, he pressed something in her palm, a cool circle.

She held it to the street light. It was a glazed ceramic, with the outline of a familiar boat with two comma-shaped sails, over a rich blue background.

"It is a Christmas ornament, from the *Hōkūleʻa* boutique. The *Star of Gladness* always finds her way, like the *iwa* bird," he said. "Keep it on you, for protection."

"I will," she said.

He put his other hand to cover hers.

"The Island will recognize you when you come back," he said. "As I will."

Then he sang, in a low whisper so the few tourists passing them did not hear.

"*Stand beside me and be my friend, oh, Hōkūleʻa, Star of Gladness.*"

"It is beautiful," she said.

"It is a song composed for the *Hōkūleʻa*, a long time ago.

She pressed herself, against him, no more longer than a few beats of his heart. Then she detached herself from the harbor of his arms, turned and almost run past the double glass doors.

Back in her pale hotel room, the paroles of the song turned ceaselessly in her head when she waited for the travel company hotline to answer.

Big Island, on the Mauna Loa flank.

The lava flow looked like gray wrinkled plastic bags filled with molasse. Except those wrinkled bags moved in slow motion, a pop of sulphur-riddled gas exploding here and there, like a sigh from the tired, abused Earth.

Everywhere, the air was suffused with brimstone and salt effluvia. Madelyn heard the hiss of water vapor produced when the two opposite elements met at the shore. White clouds rose from the encounter, looking like the clouds under a plane's wing.

White clouds she would not fly over soon. The planes were packed full. The next available seat to La Guardia would leave in three days. On Christmas.

She gripped the barrier set up to prevent visitors from trying to walk on the seemingly cool patches. She had refrained from calling Makoa and, instead, booked a two-day Hawaii Volcanoes National Park trek excursion, boat ride, guide, meals and lodging included.

And annoying vacationers.

"You would be surprised how stupid some tourists are," the man at her side said, the corners of his fleshy mouth turned up in a derogatory smile. He was in his late thirties or forties, handsome in a gym afficionado's way but clearly on the lookout for what the younger people called a *score*. "One stupid dolt tried to walk on those cushions..."

She tuned him out. There had been three or four 'hopefuls' trailing Madelyn since she undertook the Mauna Loa excursion. (Not sure about the saucy grandfather's comment on her snow-white hair, but the bumbling frat boy who 'accidentally' brushed against her one-piece swim-suit in the pool certainly was.)

Madelyn had always been proud, wearing few but good clothes, and heeding her mom's advice to stand straight and kept her hair impeccable. Now, she was garbed in her light-weight, multipockets pants and matching shirt and good walking shoes. Her hat, bought to counter the pounding sun, did not hide her silver hair.

Nevertheless, younger men hit on her like cannonballs.

She had read an article in a magazine that young women traveling alone felt like big walking targets for idle men. More than one had complained how impossible it was for them to just *enjoy* a place and relax. Madelyn pursed her lips.

It isn't only the young ones, she thought.

Nor did it happen only to the obviously beautiful ones. She had observed two middle-aged tourists in the group happily waddling around like queen bees, attended by one or two fresh-faced boys.

A bald Bezos look-alike had told Madelyn she had a willowy kind of beauty, like royalty in exile. A blond bearded man reminding her of Kurt Cobain had waxed eloquent on her firm tummy, as if he could see through her roomy shirt. She had almost retorted that, *yes, going up and down the stairs on four stories would do that*, but she did not wish to encourage more flirting.

Madelyn had told her daughter in playful tones that she was going to Hawaii looking for the three *S*, but she did not care much for one of those S, no more than being cast as a potential sugar-mom. She did not scorn the middle-aged women in the group looking for a tryst; she had been tempted herself after the divorce. But then, she had had a teenage girl to guide into adulthood.

As now, she felt her place was in her daughter's company. She tried calling from the base camp, or sending a text message. She got a short "Hi mom, I'm OK" message after a long trek on the flank of the Mauna Kea, but no way to speak to Emily.

"And they say the ancient sacrificed virgins to the goddess..."

Ignoramus, spitting up hearsay to despise the proud inhabitants! Madelyn focused her thoughts on the molasse-looking lava flow, dismissing the vain man and his cackling from her mind. Volcano factoids came to her rescue: the

Mauna Loa was a 'shield' volcano, the woman guide had said, because of the low conical shape.

It was so massive its weight depressed the Earth's crust a good eight kilometers under the ocean floor. Adding its summit's altitude of 4000 m and the distance to the sea floor, that made the Mauna Loa the highest volcano on Earth, at seventeen kilometers.

Like love, like an iceberg, only a small bit showing at the surface. Had she shown enough love for Emily?

On the forested path leading to the lava field, Madelyn had spotted red flashes through curling branches. She recognized the scarlet body and curved beak of the I'ivi bird, going for the nectar of equally rare hibiscus flowers growing from the lava.

She came back to her senses when she noticed that her group had advanced farther on the path, rounding the mouth of the volcano. She followed them, keeping her distance, keeping her spine straight, even if she wanted to droop like a willow.

The annoying hopeful's words had polluted her mind, with the image of a young girl sacrificed to the volcano. She could linger behind.

Advance past the railing, taking one step...

A shadow zipped over the gray lava flow. She lifted her eyes in time to get a glimpse of a swift silhouette, its sharp tail divided. A frigatebird, the *iwa* bird who always knew where he was going. Did she know herself?

Madelyn chased the thought, and tried to reach her

daughter, again. No answer. She left a short message, warning Emily about her advanced arrival date. She would not leave her daughter alone.

The bird veered off to the blue table of the sea, leaving her in the ashy expanse of volcanic soil.

She felt the crumpled card through the fabric of her pant, along with the cool metal of the round keepsake.

The gentle face of Makoa rose before her mind's eye. The doctor would be at home with his family. While she would be in the hotel, alone, or at the bar with a bunch of young sharks circling around her. And she would spend the whole Christmas day in the sky...

One tear escaped her eye. In the ambient heat, she was aware of it only when it sizzled on the hot rock, below the rail. She felt used, tired. This excursion was turning into a circus. She should have consulted the botanist before choosing that tour company. She couldn't endure one more day.

One more day... The disk felt cool and smooth in her palm as she pulled her cell. She called the number she had put in memory. Heart pounding, she waited until she heard the click. His warm voice filled her ear.

"Madelyn?"

Maui Island

FOUR HOURS LATER, Madelyn disembarked from the ferry, proud that she did not fell ill during the crossing from the Big Island. She had had to pay a taxi down the volcano, then catch the ferry, but it had been worth it.

Makoa was waiting at the small Maui harbor, in comfortable pants and a rather festive shirt in red and green leaves. A tall young woman that must be his daughter stood at his side.

The daughter greeted her, to Madelyn's surprise, with a *lei* of hibiscus and white flowers, smelling so good she felt at home.

"Aloha," the young woman said, with a smile that left no place for anything but a sincere welcome.

"This is Louann," he said, a proud father. "My youngest, and a marine biologist."

Louann was ebullient, her short hair bobbing as she talked.

"Dad spoke of you so well during those last days, I'm happy you decided to come."

She almost didn't.

"I, It won't be long, because I will fly off Hawaii tomorrow, so I hope I'm not..."

Before she could say *intruding*, Makoa enveloped her in his arms.

"You're not intruding, my star, never. And Kiana can't wait to meet you, as well."

She felt her whole body warming in his embrace. This time, she did not let any *proper* thought stop her from responding, a boat safely anchored in her peaceful harbor, her sails folded.

She looked up at him just as he lowered his head and, just like that, their lips met. A soft bounce at first, then their mouths met again for a longer, ardent kiss under the cloudless sky.

LOUANN HAD a firm hand on the wheel, on the winding road, her short hair flying. Madelyn was huddled against Makoa's mass like a planet, the bumps on the road echoing through his chest.

The sea was a quiet tableau of emerald and blue and violets when Louann parked the car next to a one-story wooden house adorned with a generous balcony. Another woman was waiting by the front porch, one hand holding a three- or four-year-old boy and her other hand cupping her bulging belly. No wonder their father had wanted to be with them! She looked like she could pop any minute.

"This is Kiana, with my next grandchild, I hope!"

Despite the weariness of pregnancy, the woman's smile was luminous.

"Welcome!" she said.

A smiling youth hopped past her to take Makoa's enormous suitcase.

Madelyn crossed the threshold of the house, to find a Hawaiian table set up. More heavenly cookies' smell wafted from the kitchen. It was the 24th of December, but they would not wait for midnight, because of the children and cousins. Makoa'a sister and brother had joined them, with their spouses, and the kitchen sounded like a musical battle of utensils.

"My dear star, I have things to attend. I'll leave you to my daughters. You should survive," he added with a wink.

Kiana seized a cushion and threw it at her father.

"Ooh, go already, you big oaf!"

Madelyn felt at ease with Kiana, who enjoyed a reprieve due to her condition. She sipped green tea with honey in a ancient china cup, and immersed herself in the Maui house. They had hung ribbons and flowers to the rafters, but few Hawaiians cut a fir tree to underline Christmas.

But joy was everywhere she lay her eyes on. Beauty in the pale wood and warm colors, the rattan chairs, the cousin's telling fun stories, the hanging silk tapestries, the rafters running overhead to meet the pillars supporting the straw roof, the golden round faces of the children...

There was just one missing.

A lime-green laptop landed on the coffee table. Makoa sat on her other side, opening the computer. He tapped a very long password (good) and started opening a session.

Kiana crossed her arms.

"Hay dad, I thought I said, no technology!"

"Kia, it's an emergency," he said.

"What are you doing?" Madelyn asked, as the high-pitched scream of a session rose.

"The Wi-Fi is strong in this house," he said, in a charming Yoda style.

She almost dropped her teacup when a familiar face appeared, her dark raven hair well combed, her eyes shining, her smile infectious. Emily!

Behind her daughter, she guessed a cozy restaurant, with checkered tablecloths and dimmed lights. The ambiance was joyful, with laugher and clinking of glasses. Of course, there was a five hours lag, so it would be well past midnight there.

"Emily, where are you? Are you OK? Your meds? Who's that man with you?"

The bearish man besides her spluttered something.

"Mooom!" Emily said, flustered. "You don't have to worry about me! I can take care of myself, and Rafe is a veterinary. We are celebrating Christmas at a friend's restaurant. We met just after I left the airport."

She had no idea how such an encounter could have happened, but the bear-like man looked the soft type.

"Hello," Makoa said, leaning on her shoulder.

"Oh, hi, mister Kalama! T'was good of you to call me."

Flabbergasted, Madelyn looked from her virtual daughter to the man she had come to love.

"I do not remember giving you my home number, professor," she said.

He shrugged.

"Well, I had to dig around a bit in the directory."

Emily cut in.

"Mom, as soon as you called him from that volcano, he called me at the flat. He told me you were worried sick over me and wanted to cut your vacations short. So we arranged to this call."

The next few minutes, Emily filled her with the news, and Rafe, who looked like a decent type. They exchanged warm wishes, and Emily added. "And pleeease, mom, stay as long as you need!"

LATER, when all was said and done, children at bed and plates washed and put away, Makoa guided Madelyn on the long balcony overlooking the slope descending to the sea. She wore a light pareo over her swimsuit. He had shaken off the pants and festive shirt.

The evening air brought a cool breeze, and silence, the birds themselves tucked for the night. A hot bath was gently bubbling, uncovered, its lights toned down to an pale blue. And a mistletoe ball was hanging from a rafter. She couldn't have wished for a better Christmas Eve.

Million of stars filled the sky, a sight she would never get tired of.

"Where's Arcturus?" she asked, taking off the pareo, the prospect of entering the hot tub with a man and doing improper things quite enticing.

Makoa Kalama pointed at a twinkling, red-hued point. Almost right over their heads.

"Like you," he said, "the Star of Gladness is the brightest in the sky."

He took her hand as if it was the most fragile crystal on Earth, and waded in the pool with her, slow as lava. The hot bubbling water made Madelyn feel like champagne, all the worries dissolving in bliss, her silver hair floating free. She leaned against his body, her harbor, her eyes turned up.

All over them, stars of gladness shone like benevolent eyes.

Hōkūleʻa !

THE KEPT-IN'S CHRISTMAS EVE

JUDY UPHILL SWALLOWED a sinful tumbler of vodka-laced eggnog to pacify her grumbling stomach. She shouldn't drink, but her strict stuntwoman diet, coupled with the exertion of tidying up a two-story mansion and cooking the perfect Christmas Eve dinner, had conspired to lower her defenses.

After a guilt-ridden glance toward the front door, she washed and put away the goblet in the glass cupboard, fumbling with the porcelain latch. The tiny alcohol content was already melting her insides like soft caramel.

Judy leaned against the fifteen-foot granite counter of the gazillion-dollar designer's kitchen, breathing in the aroma of almond cookies baking in the oversized oven. She had a mountain of chores to finish before Porter came back.

She gazed through the sink window. At the dead,

snowless grass. At the sky, its stars hidden by the light pollution. Only one blinking red dot moved in the emptiness, a plane packed with last-minute travelers going to their families' homes.

Judy's own emptiness clogged her throat. How she missed the glittering sky over her parents' cottage!

The almond cookies still needed ten minutes.

Judy flopped on the sprawling living room couch, sending up a few pale strands of cat hair. She looked at the crystal chandelier hanging from the twelve-foot ceiling, then to the medieval-sized foyer facing her, its smile of blue gas flames protected by a metal grid. A black-tiled ledge protected the illusion. Almost touching the ledge, stood the requisite Christmas tree, its artificial limbs bent under pounds of ornaments and lights, its point topped by a glass angel.

Judy stretched, clad in her go-to charcoal-gray yoga pants and an orange Tee sporting the ninja silhouette of her gym's logo. Faint traces of Porter's Cologne lingered on the couch's black leather...

Handsome in a lean, fortyish fashion with silvering hair, Porter was as smart and witty as befitted a talented scriptwriter pursued by all major movie producers. (All but one: he had pissed off Spielberg last year, for some obscure reason.)

Porter had been considerate and fun with her, his fame a glowing halo. Smitten, Judy had moved in with him in a week, marveling at a kitchen her dad would have died for, at the fairytale foyer, at the sparkling chandelier, at the room-sized bathrooms and at the walled garden, large enough to practice her combat choreographies...

A HIGH-PITCHED YOWL, followed by a frantic yapping, called Judy from the soft depths of the couch's embrace. She registered a patter of nails on kitchen tiles, then more hissing and yowling.

Still squabbling, she thought.

A loud crystal crash rang her inner alarm full tilt. The young woman opened her eyes to a nightmare.

Porter's ten-foot Christmas tree was wobbling as Mad and Madder, as she called his cats, chased each other around its tripod base. Glittering pieces of the glass angel, dislodged from its perch, lay on the regal foyer's tiles.

McCoy, Judy's caramel-and-white basset hound, was chasing the cats, his short legs sinking in the jumble of pearly white electric lines linking the tree to the mural connector.

An angry hiss from behind the base sent McCoy flying to the opposite corner of the living room, yelping as his head knocked the leg of a glass display case. The *Marvel Special Edition* action figures standing inside toppled over each other in lurid, un-heroic positions.

While the black-and-white cat played with the electric lines, the tortoiseshell jumped all claws out in the lower branches, clearly aiming for a vintage tear-shaped ornament. The devilish creature's wild grappling unbalanced the tree, who tipped forward with a furious jingling.

Muttering a curse, Judy launched herself from the couch, stretching her arms to catch the tree before it hit the immaculate carpet.

The twenty-eight-years-old possessed the trained reflexes of a professional stunt double, but the exhaustion of tidying, cooking and baking tons of biscuits, plus her contractual weight obligation (and tumbler of vodka eggnog), had messed those reflexes.

Hundreds of hard plastic needles scored her bare arms as Judy grabbed the central pole protected by looped tinsels, more needles and twisted electric lines. The corner of the foyer's ledge hit her left elbow. The sharp pain of the impact would not be worth a mention on a shooting set, not like a bad fall in a combat scene.

The immense tree was now leaning on the young woman at an angle, its taut needles pressing against her orange Tee. Her head in the needles, Judy smelled the false fir scent Porter had sprayed on the branches.

The tree, with kilograms of crystal globes, vintage ornaments, false gift boxes, hundreds of white LED lights, weighted as much as a median adult. Still, Judy managed to break its fall.

What she couldn't stop, though, was the rain of ornaments dislodged by her quick action. She winced as more crystal pieces crashed on the hard tiles of the foyer.

She pushed the tree back to its upright position. Porter would be fuming when he saw the wreckage of his vintage tear-shaped ornaments. His doting parents would raise their noses and *tsssk* at her.

At her, the genius scriptwriter's kept-in girlfriend.

A shot of anger burnt through her, like a too-strong spirit. Judy turned to the pair of culprits, now serenely lounging by the bay window, licking their paws.

Mad was a black and white lady, her immaculate face and pink nose giving her an angelic air. Madder was a tortoiseshell with a clear penchant for antics, as she demonstrated by hunting dangling ornaments in the tree.

Poor McCoy looked at his mistress from under the Marvel figurines display case with its toppled superheroes, his sad brown eyes questing affection.

The basset and the territorial cats did not get along on most days. Christmas Eve was no exception.

Fists on her hips, Judy cast the duo of felines a withering stare that would have been any aspiring actress's dream.

"You," she said, "will not get the Tuna Special this evening!"

It was an empty threat, because as soon as he came back from the airport, Porter would spoil them rotten.

JUDY CROUCHED to caress her diminutive basset, his pendulous ears and skin folds giving his face the sad puppy look she fell in love with at the pound.

She checked his brown eyes for any redness, and guided the dog's uneven steps down the basement's stairs. McCoy's wicker basket lay next to a pair of washing-drying machines with windows like spaceship portholes. At each laundry, Judy had to reassure her dog, unnerved by the sloshing noise and the clothes spinning behind the porthole.

Basset hounds were renowned as calm and placid, but the volunteer at the Portland Animal Rescue shelter had told Judy that McCoy had been neglected by his former masters. He had a gimp leg and jumped at sudden noises.

After a last look at her companion, his sad puppy eyes raised over the basket rim, Judy scampered upstairs to survey the disaster. It looked as if an army of miniature trolls had attacked the tree and rained silver fragments of ornaments on the floor. The thick carpet had cushioned the fall of the upper ornaments, but too many had crashed on the flat stones near the base and bounced away. Brillant shards peeked from the threads of the creamy carpet.

She needed to vacuum the carpet before the in-laws came, because Porter's brother and sister-in-law had two picture-perfect children. And put those Marvel figurines back up.

And *what* was giving off this burnt smell? Oh.

Judy ran to the kitchen where her batch of what should have been almond cookies were consuming themselves.

She scrambled for mitts and pulled off the oven a tray of dark circles. Leaning on the cold granite counter, she set to scrape off the blackened husks. She was wrangling the scorched remains in the Garburator sink hole when a nerve-wracking ululation seared her ears.

Judy climbed on the central island to reach the Camembert-shaped smoke detector, and tap it shut. Panting, she looked up the hour: seven and ten.

Time to pull the pre-cooked dead bird from its wraps and put it in the oven, to reheat. Last year, Porter had hired a catering service. This year, he had opted for a homely DIY feel. Which meant, a Judy-Do-It feel. She had willingly gone along with it, in the hopes of getting his family's approbation.

After the turkey, she got into the pantry to pull out a blue egg-shaped vacuum cleaner, hitting her already sore elbow in the process.

Great, now my coordination's failing! she thought.

THE CUTE EGG-SHAPED vac-cleaner overheated and gave up the ghost in minutes. Only the bi-weekly cleaning crew's power machines could remove embedded glass shards. Judy claimed a white kitchen bag and walked back to the living room.

As she scooped up the bigger shards from the carpet, she felt overtaken by an impression of being a stranger. She missed her one-bedroom flat, three streets from the river. But she had rescinded the rent when she moved into Porter's lavish house.

Everything around her felt off: the too-dark leather couch with the imprint of her lean body across it; the pale khaki walls; the thick cream-colored carpet, twinkling with smaller shards. The mural gold-plated clock with Roman numbers ordered from Switzerland.

Even the fairy-tale stone foyer was spooking her now. The gridiron barrier was pulled shut so neither cats nor incoming children would take into their cute little heads to explore the cavernous space behind the false logs. The chimney trapdoor was shut, too, to prevent cold air from invading the living room.

She was getting more and more of this sense of not *belonging*, even if she had loved the place: the master bedroom done in classic browns and blues with the requisite four posters bed, walk-in closet and tall mirror; the study lined with floor-to-ceiling bookshelves and a mahogany writing desk with the laptop.

Judy liked cooking in the well-equipped kitchen (with a vacuum sealing machine!) But it was torture to sit at the table with a meager salad and beans plate to respect her contractual weight requirement, while Porter, tall and slim like his mother, ate like an ogre.

Only the den in the basement felt like home, with

McCoy's wicker basket in view while she jogged on the rolling carpet. But she couldn't rehearse her choreography there, with the washing/drying spaceship and Porter's exercise machines taking most of the space.

SHE WAS STILL PICKING up shards off the carpet when she heard a tinny orchestral rendition of *Con Te Partiro*. Her canary yellow cell was dancing in circles on the polished wood of the side table, on its max vibration setting.

Now, what? she thought, her mood tittering between rage and zen-like acceptance of life's little annoyances.

She didn't have the luxury of ignoring a call, not this evening. It could be Porter telling her his parents' plane had not landed yet, or asking about the dinner, or it could be the studio. Or...

She hadn't spoken with her parents in years. She envisioned the affectionate pair decorating their tree, going at the local Mom-and-Pop restaurant to meet friends.

She'd invite them here, but they lived on the West Coast and had stopped traveling since the pandemic struck. Worst, neither her Dad nor Mom were big Internet users.

None had called since she moved with Porter three years ago. Maybe she had disappointed them by choosing a stunt woman career. Her brother also kept radio silence.

She ran to the side table.

"'Lo?" she gasped.

She should have drunk mineral water instead of that egg-nog.

A raucous voice exploded at the other end.

"Judy baby, the shooting is a go! But it starts next Monday."

Mighty Al, from the *Champion Den Studio*. He had been a stunt double in his youth, and forty years later he looked the part of an aging Sylvester Stallone. Now he managed the lesser-known operatives in a movie production, body doubles and stuntmen.

"But, Al, I was supposed to have two weeks!" she said, failing to hide the annoyance from her voice.

Mighty Al poured a torrent of words, ending with a convocation. Judy was too tired to protest.

She had signed the retainer contract when she was single and unemployed, for a good fee. She had to study movie projects specs and train to get her combat choreographies down pat. She also modelled the lead actress' costumes for light measurements before the actual shooting.

And...

Judy pinched a centimeter of body fat at her waist. She was lean and muscular, but still eleven pounds over the lead actress's current weight. Judy had counted on the week following the New Year Eve feeding frenzy to get back to her contractual weight and polish her combat scenes.

She also needed those days to work out her relationship with Porter.

Too many little things didn't add up. She played hostess for guests who only saw her as his kept-in girlfriend. Porter had not shown any inclination toward deepening their commitment. The romantic *will-you-marry-me* scene Judy had envisioned at the start of their whirlwind romance had not materialized yet.

She loved his wit, but this agile tongue of his could get mean in a flash whenever he choose to. Like the last time she had lobbed the commitment question at him.

"Do you want a ring?" he had said, with that snarky tone he usually reserved for critics he didn't care about.

When she had gasped aloud, stricken, he had dialed down the sarcasm scale.

"You know I don't like to be pushed into marriage," he said in a soothing tone, before shutting himself in the study.

Judy was no husband chaser, despite her biological clock clicking louder. But she had been peeved when she learned that Porter had waited a full year before telling his parents about his new girlfriend.

Her meetings with the pair had been dry, his parents being so well-off they jetted where they wanted. No harsh words were exchanged, but the way his peroxided mother consulted her phone, the indifferent look his balding father cast, the perfunctory compliments. (*Oh, you're a stunt girl? How original!*)

A fiancée Judy was definitely not. At least, she was, by the joined efforts of three generations of Uphill women and men, a fair cook.

Mighty Al's scraggly voice piped in her thoughts.

"Hey Jude! You' listening? So get your gear ready for Monday!"

She nodded. "Okay, I'll..."

The line cut before she was finished nodding. Mighty Al was a busy man, which meant, in the industry, no call lasted a second longer than needed. Unless he hit on her, which would bring another kind of hell.

THE SWISS MURAL clock chimed nine when Judy finished removing the shards she could feel with her fingers. She had a good chunk of free time before having to shower, change and greet Porter's family. Time she could use. Her gym was closed today, but the living room space was perfect.

Judy pushed the coffee table against the leather couch. She stretched her limbs to prepare her body for explosive action. Her combat scene lasted two minutes and a forty seconds.

She tied up her sneakers and stood, facing the window and the pair of cats.

No snow. The front lawn, the three wire-framed reindeers grazed on the dead grass. The red dot of a plane was moving slowly in the otherwise empty sky.

Judy closed her eyes; breathed in; out. Counted the beats in her head.

Then she launched herself across the room, pirouetting, swiveling, fists shooting off as she battled invisible adversaries left and right. *The Mooks*, she thought, lower-rank baddies that the female character would beat without difficulty to imprint her skills in the spectator's mind.

She had four *mooks* to dispatch, one every thirty seconds. If the doubles playing the mooks were as well prepared, their scene could be wrapped sooner.

Her pace slowed down after the fourth "mook". She jumped over his (imaginary) body to prod forward, her head swiveling left and right to check the location (a dark warehouse) for any sign of additional danger.

Judy stepped toward the ledge of the foyer, executed a quarter turn to the bay window (a noise in the scene draws the heroine's attention). Suddenly, her head whipped back (as a boss baddie's karate-chop clobbered her character) and she collapsed in a boneless heap on the living room carpet.

The 'boneless' posture actually required more efforts, her body twisted in a sexy pose: face to the foyer, knees to the window.

As a body double, Judy would stay inert for ten seconds (that would be sheared off the final cut), so the lead actress could match the position for the close-up of her unconscious figure. On the thick carpet (there would be none in the movie studio), the falling was not too bad, except for her lancing elbow and a budding headache.

At the eleventh second, Judy unfolded from the carpet and jumped to her starting point.

She went through the whole routine twice, without a hitch.

At the fourth iteration, she overcompensated the last move by a few inches and flopped too close to the foyer. The angular stone ledge grazed her brow.

Pain and dizziness launched her headache into a pounding boss-baddie level. She felt her brow with trembling fingers: no bleeding, but the upcoming purple bump would annoy the make-up artist next Monday.

Cursing the vodka-laced eggnog, Judy rolled on her back and kept still, hoping she didn't nurse a concussion. Everyone knew of a sports star or an actor who ignored a headache, only to turn up dead the next day.

She closed her eyes, breathed in, out, in...

A gust of arctic air blew from the chimney sending goosebumps on her arms. The chimney trap must have fallen open. But the cold receded, replaced by the warm aromas of chocolate cookies, fruitcake and gingerbread (that she definitively did not cook!)

Then a deep, cavernous voice hollered out.

"By my pixies, are you wounded?"

JUDY OPENED her eyes to a vision in scarlet red and fluffy whites.

She bounced back, fists raised.

The chimney intruder wore a Santa outfit, several sizes over extra-large, a dark belt with a silver buckle, a red cap topped by a white tennis ball-sized pompom. White gloves and boots completed the picture.

Break-outs happened in posh neighborhoods, especially in the holidays when most residents flew under more clement skies. Because he had left Judy cooking inside the house, Porter had not set the sophisticated 12-points alarm system.

This false Santa was not the first thug using a disguise to get in a house.

Judy took the stance her self-defense instructor taught her at the gym, legs slightly apart, one in front of the other, body turned, knees flexed. Her eyes surveyed her adversary's body to find vulnerable points.

Which was not that easy when a formidable belly hung over the family jewels, and a thick, flowing white beard hid both neck and solar plexus.

That left the eyes, a pair of baby blue marbles creased with a web of amused lines, behind a pair of silver-rimmed glasses. The intruder looked old enough to be her grandfather when she was a child.

A very *big* grandad. Those baby blue marbles hovered at well over six feet.

My God! she thought.

How could this giant swoop down a chimney that was, at the most, thirteen inches wide? With his expansive belly and height, the Santa guy would weight about three hundred and fifty pounds!

He could eat at a Heart-Attack Grill for free, a cynical part of her thought.

The burglar adjusted his fine-rimmed glasses to get a better look at Judy, and that's when she noticed how his gloves were an immaculate white, how his red coat with fur trimmings glowed like satin. Even if the chimney had been wide enough, the soot-grimed bricks of the conduit would have stained his costume. The grid was still in place...

Judy chided herself. With the 12-points alarm disarmed, he must have used another way for breaking and entering... Her eyes locked on the red canvas bag, almost as big as he was, hanging from a shoulder. A very *full* bag. Was he already robbing the upper stair rooms while she trained?

"Who are you? How did you get here?" she asked, keeping the fear from her voice.

The intruder exploded in a rumbling laughter, his belly shaking like a jelly bowl, his eyes squeezing shut. A small bell hidden in the pompom atop his cap rang.

"Two funny questions," he said.

His jolly tone did not reassure Judy. He made no aggressive move, as he lowered the huge bag on the carpet, its contents jiggling in a soft whisper of cardboard boxes.

"I, I can call the police," she said, keeping her combat stance.

Where was her cell? Beads of sweat dripped along her spine.

The man disguised as Santa inclined his head on the side, the bell pompom still ringing. His baby blue eyes peered at her through the round lenses, as if she was an interesting specimen. A green flash dashed around the fine rims, maybe a metal reflection.

"Why are you afraid of, *Judith*?" he asked.

His voice was at odds with his incredible mass, low and soft as her grand-father's had been.

Judy's fists clenched so hard her nails would pierce her skin if she had let them grow. *Afraid?*

"Oh, let's see," she answered in a droll tone. "First you know my name. That's makes you a stalker!"

Porter's wit and success had brought him as many rivals and bitter enemies as friends. Whoever had decided to loot his study's safe or steal his manuscripts would know all about his kept-in girlfriend.

She bit her lower lip.

Kept-in.

This wasn't what Judy had wanted in life. She was proud of her stunts, but Porter had told her more than once she didn't need new gigs now that he provided for both of them.

The genius scriptwriter's girlfriend.

A rumbling *hohoho* shook her thoughts like feathers in a very fluffy pillow.

A soft, uneven paddling sounded on the carpet. McCoy had come to investigate, his lumbering gait unmistakable.

"Oh, but I know all the names!" the false Santa said.

So that's how you play it, right? Judy thought.

"And who's been naughty or *niiice*," she sang, the tune so familiar.

"Oh, I know *you've* been nice, my girl! Doing your homework an all..."

The huge Santa's voice petered off as his eyes alighted on the mangled tree, with the remaining broken ornaments littering the underside, the streamers like silver snakes. Moreover, three branches had been skewered, leaving glaring gaps in the ornaments ranks.

"My, my!" he said. "Methink's someone has been naughty here, heh?"

Judy followed his gaze to the window. Both cats sat on their haunches, staring at the man, mesmerized. McCoy had found a spot under the coffee table, his droopy head resting on his paws.

"Not nice, Beatrice and Bally, to hound this poor McCoy!"

Dear God! To Porter, McCoy was 'my girlfriend's dog' when he entertained at home.

"How do you know my dog's name?" she asked.

A stalker would know the cats' names, but it was impossible that someone had followed Judy five years ago in the animal shelter of another city. She had been distraught after a break-up, and needed a faithful companion.

The Santa bent over to pat McCoy on his head. The move in such an enormous body transformed him into a red ball. She picked up a delicious aroma of the maple sugar pie her dad cooked, long ago. Where did it come from?

"Hey, buddy, take it easy. I know you're a good dog."

McCoy was too shy to warm up to strangers, and did not even endure Porter's touch. But this total weirdo got instantly accepted, if Judy could believe the soft whimpers and the tongue lapping the stranger's hand.

She brushed her palms together, suffused with a tingling hope, like when she was a wee girl. Could this gentle giant be the real McCoy?

But no. She had stopped believing long ago.

Do the math. If Santa somehow found his way in this house —this childless, heartless house—it was impossible to do *billions* of houses, appartements, huts, lean-to, caverns, refugee camps, in the same night.

Then another detail came up.

"It's not even midnight," she said, ignoring the tiny hammers pounding in her head. "And, well, there's no children living here."

He rose from his crouch, the tip of his cap brushing the

lower curves of the chandelier. Really, this weird Santa could play basketball if he had been leaner.

"My work begins way before midnight," he said.

His eyes, paler than ice, shone behind the round lenses as if a flood projector stood behind Judy.

"There was a child waiting for me, in *this* house," he said.

Judy pulled a bit of pluckiness from a hidden pocket.

"I'm not a child anymore, big guy," she said, words spilling fast. "I'm waiting for my boyfiend to come back!"

His eyes, so jolly a few minutes ago, became shrouded in mist.

"My, my, such desire to get ensnared by a *fiend*."

That's when Judy realized what she had unwittingly said.

"A telling lapsus," the Santa guy said.

"No, no, I love Porter, I do!" Judy countered. Her voice sounded meek to her ears. "But, I just wish, that..."

She caught herself in time. She had been lulled by his grandfatherly act, and about to blurt her pain to a stranger! The huge Santa looked around him.

"But you feel trapped."

Judy looked at the Swiss clock. Ten thirty. She felt a panic rise. How could more than one hour have passed? Her concussion, was it worsening?

She cast an anxious glance at the door. Any moment, Porter's BMW would turn in the cobbled entrance...

"Look, whoever you are, you should go, really," she said. "Porter won't appreciate, he'll call the cops..."

She raised her palms and pushed against the red ball of a belly, trying to get him to the back door. It felt like plunging in a soft mattress, but that softness hid an immovable object.

She felt like a child. And those sweet scents swirling around filled her with a longing she had not felt in ages. For home, for simplicity, for her grandma's cakes, for her dad's maple sugar pies.

"Judy," he said, "I have something to show you. But first, let's tidy up this place."

He pulled off his red cap. More white hair tumbled down, long and curly. He shook the cap. The jingle bell in the pompom rang, high and pure.

Blue dust fell on the floor. Not dust: motes of lights, twirling around the living room, brushing the couch, the coffee table with the books, the display shelves, the special edition figurines...

Shiny shards jetted off Judy's white plastic bag; many others she had missed, barely bigger than a speck, rose from the carpet to rebuild intact balls of glass. The tinsels' snakes slithered up the tree. The reassembled tear-shaped vintage ornament took back its place, and the angel at the top was whole again, wings outstretched.

The cats zoomed from the windowsill, so fast Judy would not believe her eyes. McCoy did not rise from his spot, his brown eyes twinkling under his droopy lids.

That's when she heard noise in the kitchen. Another intruder?

Judy stepped closer.

A tall woman was rolling a pie crust, clad in a sunset-blue dress and apron, snowy hair pulled up in a bun. She sprinkled the cookies, then turned to the oven.

Her twig-like arms reached inside to pull a steaming plate of turkey, *without using mitts*!

The elderly woman put the plate down. Her delicate fingers, unburnt, palms rosy, were coated with flour dust. Shiny motes of yellow light, like tiny stars, rose from the fabric of her blue dress.

Sensing Judy's gaze, the crone smiled, her teeth indistinct under a soft light that seemed to come from inside her head. She did not wear any make-up, not even lipstick, but her eyes and mouth were sharply delineated.

"Do not worry, child," she said, her dark, dark eyes shining like onyx. "Everything will be fine."

She had a soft, ageless, peaceful voice. She did not look at all like Judy's grandma, who had been petite and roundish, but there was something familiar in the face. That same dedication to everything she was doing, like the cupcakes currently cooling on the counter.

The blue-garbed fairy cast a glance at the twirling motes in the living room. Her lips pursed in mock anger.

"That dear husband, always showing off!"

The affection under the words hinted at a person constitutionally unable of screaming in anger or hurling verbal abuse at anyone. Judy clutched her arms, fingers digging in her biceps, feeling a rush of emotion laying waste inside her.

Tears welled in her eyes, spilling on her cheeks.

"That's what called me here," Santa said.

"Klaus, you could have done it without her knowing," his wife said, her flour-covered fists on her thin hips.

Behind her, a procession of plates sailed through the air, trailing the best almond cookie odors of all times, and then, oh, was it a spice chocolate cake, and lemon scones? All plates settled like UFOs on the tablecloth adorned with ribbons and mistletoes, sugar canes everywhere. The good cutlery was out, already, borne out by a spattering of brilliant stars.

The fairy had set the table for Porter's parents and his brother's family, but... She counted again.

One place was missing.

Hers.

Tears streaked her cheeks, as she fell on her rump in a sorry heap. McCoy padded close and licked her hands.

WHEN JUDY BLINKED off the torrent, the big Santa had his red cap back on. He bent over the old cook and deposited a puckered-lips smack on her crown of snowy hair.

"You won't get away with it, you know that, dear?

There's rules," the woman was saying, her voice still soft as silk.

"Oh, darling, her soul was crying loud and clear..."

Whose soul? Judy thought, her hands on McCoy's warm pelt.

"Like the rest of humanity," his wife replied, with a benevolent smile. "But that's why I married you, you big, bleeding-heart oaf!"

"I'm sure the Boss will understand."

The Boss word snapped Judy out of her misery. All this time, moping for herself. She got up, pushing the headache at the back of her mind.

"Yes," she said, battling the ball of grief in her throat. "You should care for all the others on the planet, there's so much poverty everywhere..."

And abandoned animals, she added for herself.

A loud thump, like a giant's robot's hand hitting the roof, echoed through the house. The cutlery and glasses in every cupboards clinked, and the superheroes figurines toppled again.

"Ah," both Santa and his wife said, in such perfect unison that Judy was reminded of her parents.

"What is it?" Judy asked.

The Santa emitted a bark of laughter,

"No worry!" he said.

Looking at the bay window, Judy sucked in a happy breath. Fluffy white flurries landed on the lawn, making a velvety carpet lit up in deep violets and soft reds. Those colors couldn't come from the streetlights.

And, oh, was there *four* tall trees planted on the street?

She gasped when a Soyouz-sized sphere lowered itself to the window, half of its curve glowing a deep carmine at the limit of the infrareds.

Judy didn't see anything besides that incredible ball, and the two jets of white steam under it.

The fairy woman in blue chuckled.

"Well, see how your bragging trickles on poor Rudolph?"

"Almost done," the Santa—Klaus or Claus? —said.

When Judy wrenched her attention from the glowing red sphere, the living room stood as untouched, her white plastic bag out of view. The food smells were so wonderful she felt ready to jump with glee. Mrs. Klaus (Judy had opted in her head for this name) was laying down a slip of paper next to the red napkins artistically folded.

"And what was it you wanted to show me?" she asked.

The big red Santa got redder in the face.

His wife lifted her hand to tap his rounded shoulder.

"Now, dear, this needs a gentle touch. Let me do it."

Her flour-covered fingers touched Judy's throbbing elbow. The pain ebbed out. As did the pounding under her cranium. She closed her eyes, grateful to the odd couple.

∼

WHEN SHE OPENED HER EYES, she was not in the kitchen but standing in Porter's study, with the neat rows of books and the writing desk.

The fairy's long fingers tapped the laptop keys so fast they blurred, sending up a cloud of flour powder. Somehow, Mrs. Klaus had hacked Porter's password (which was not "password" but a very convoluted sentence). Snowy strands of hair had fallen loose from her bun.

"There, my dear. This concerns you."

Judy bent over the gentle crone's shoulder to read the email displayed on the screen. It was a bullet list of instructions to an ISP server tech, so that any letter or email from Judy's mother, father, brother would be deleted. Even her yellow phone, a gift from him, had been rigged to reject any attempt at communication from family members.

Her knees wobbled as if she had received a blow from a Boss-level villain. She slapped one palm on the desk's wooden surface for support. Her voice was a whisper.

"Why? Why would he do that?"

The fairy fingers blurred again on the keyboard. Another list of emails appeared. Private emails. Judy couldn't read the content, but the subject lines were adamant.

Very private emails.

"Maybe for his research...," she said, but she did not believe her own words.

The addressee was a younger woman Judy had met in his circles. An up-and-coming writer, full of promises.

A cupcake crumbled in soggy crumbs inside her thoracic cage. Judy had been right to think she didn't belong here. She had been cut off, smothered.

Kept-in.

"He has gotten addicted to the flavor of success," Mrs. Klaus said. "You were a bouquet on his lapel."

She traced in mid-air a blue outline of a blooming flower. Then the petals wrinkled and fell.

Judy swallowed.

"I feel so, so..."

Defeated. Betrayed.

She couldn't stay in this house, his house, anymore. Nor could poor clumsy McCoy. But she had no place to stay in this city where all their friends were *his* friends. And her parents, oh, what would they think of their ungrateful daughter?

And will I ever be ready for my choreography?

Petal-soft fingers brushed her forearm. Just as swift, she was back in the living room. Snow was now piling up under the four new columns. Klaus was setting colorful wrapped boxes under the tree.

"For the children," he said, winking.

"I don't think they believe in... you," Judy said, finally acknowledging Santa as himself.

He proffered a box wrapped in tiny fir trees on a red background. The label under the red ribbon read: 'from Judy'.

"That's the reverse of what many parents do!" she said, a tiny, edgy smile on her lips.

Mrs. Klaus strode closer. Her loose silver hair had reformed in a very neat bun. She pointed at the envelope on the table.

"And this note is also from your hand, child."

"But I didn't write anything."

"The note says that you are grateful for the time spent here, learning how to care for house and friends. But now, you are needed somewhere else and wish them well."

As the blue fairy spoke these words, the truth settled in Judy's mind like an angel snow print. She knew in her heart she wouldn't stay in that plush mansion. She looked at the Swiss clock.

"Ten past eleven!" she read.

Even if she caught a plane, she could never be with her parents in time.

Santa clapped his hands in a playful sound.

"What would you say you hitch a ride with us to see your folks?" he asked.

"My f-folks? But they live in..."

She fell silent as the Soyouz-sized bubble lowered itself again, misting the tempered glass. McCoy let out a joyful bark, as if the basset had recognized a friend. She had forgotten that her visitors had their special means of transportation.

"W-well," Judy said, nonplussed. "I still have to pack my things..."

A *whoosh* of displaced air interrupted her. A door on the second level slammed shut. Then her backpack, filled to the rim, sat at her feet. Her *booted* feet. She undid the clasps to examine the contents.

Santa's wife had packed in a split-second exactly the things Judy would have chosen herself... after two or three grueling hours.

Her hands went over the fat layer on her middle. *Maybe I could train at home, in their basement,* she thought. A half-thought formed in her mind. *Lose those eleven pounds...*

The graceful crone's lips formed this adorable pout that normally only young women got away with, while her fingers played in her husband's beard.

"Please, please, my sweet child, don't heed those insane standards! I won't exert any magic toward social conformity."

Judy felt herself go red in the face. Her hands left her belly to cover her heart.

"Oh, I, I didn't...," she blurt, but she trailed off, remembering her half-formed thought.

Compassion filled the older woman's dark eyes.

"Should I have rejected my Klaus because he didn't have a gladiator's body with the requisite six-pack? Should he have ignored me because I didn't have those lush maidenly curves?"

A big red arm encircled the thin shoulders.

"Hoho-ho! My sweet cupcake, your beauty never ceases

to amaze me!" Santa said in his affectionate, rumbling voice, sending a cinnamon-scented breath.

His wife gave him a playful nudge. "Hush, you big bear! And get the sled ready."

She turned to Judy, who was wrestling herself in her coat and adjusting the straps of her backpack.

"Sweetie, just do your best, do what you love. And leave the rest to settle as it may."

A thump, louder, sounded from the roof. Santa booming voice responded.

"Coming, Rudolph!"

Then his body broke in a thousand red satin balls, passing through the grid bars, disappearing up the chimney.

"Take my hand," the blue fairy said.

Judy's fingers gingerly closed over the thin fingers, still daubed with flour.

FLYING WAS a lot like sledding around the lake, the coverlet drawn to her chin.

Bells shook and jiggled from the team of house-sized reindeers pawing the air. A red beam at the front searched the landscape, a landscape that flowed under the clear skies. Where those white peaks passing under them the Rockies?

McCoy, safe on her lap, barked at the moon crescent. They were flying so high the curvature of the planet showed. Judy should be freezing or asphyxiating or pierced by cosmic rays, but Mrs. Klaus told her the sled carried its own protective bubble.

Suddenly, Judy saw hundreds of reindeer-pulled sleds flying left and right. Red-clad, big-bellied Santas held the reins, their jolly faces showing every skin tone between ivory and ebony... one was even driving, no, flying a 53-foot-long delivery truck!

She bubbled with the urge to talk, to tell she understood. Mrs. Klaus, draped in a satin coat and a pill-box hat covering her white bun, patted the young woman's shoulder.

The gesture brought forward, in clear details, her grandma doing the same after each visit. The little girl had taken her for granted, then. Her grandmother had known that each visit could be the last. Judy felt a pang inside.

"I miss her," she said, her voice covered by the mad jingling.

Mrs. Klaus spoke, her voice soft as warm chocolate.

"I miss my grandma, too," she said. "But she had left me so much knowledge, and recipes!"

Judy nodded and sank a little more in the thick fur wraps, drinking the luminous presence of Santa's fairy wife. She closed her eyes, exhausted; maybe the bubble around the sled leaked oxygen.

The bells' silvery voices rang louder, louder as she fell weightlessly through a mass of clouds.

JUDY OPENED HER EYES. The sky was clear, the stars so neat she could almost grab one. She was propped against a metal pole, McCoy a ball of warmth on her folded knees.

She should be freezing, teeth chattering, but the cold air did not bite. No moisture trapped in her clothes, no sweat runnel tracing her back, her feet were numb but warm. It was as if the winter had taken a pause.

It must be close to midnight. She wondered what Porter's family would make of the miraculous dinner and the presents she had left. Maybe by an effect of distance, she did not care much. She guessed Mad and Madder would be well-cared for, one redeeming quality in Porter.

Judy searched the celestial tapestry for some tangible proof she hadn't dreamed this encounter. She found a brilliant point moving north, most probably a satellite.

It flashed a quick red and zoomed out.

Judy brushed the snow from her yoga pants and stood up, feeling the pack settle on her back. The pole she had leant against supported a little mailbox in the shape of a house, with a front door to slip envelopes in, and all windows at the right places. Her dad's work. You pulled the roof open to get the mail.

Behind the mailbox sat the original model, the snow shoveled in small mountain ranges along the entrance path. She could hear the TV going on, filling the windows with a bluish glow.

Judy walked to the door with a welcoming crown of fir branches, McCoy shambling on her talons in the snow. She picked up the basset hound. Mom would be so amazed!

Hot tears came out, carrying away the last dregs of her headache. She had a hunch the fairy wife of Klaus was right. She would talk to her parents, to her brother, mend the hole her absence had left.

She would do her best, practice the combat choreographies she loved so, set her limits with Big Al. Even if that gig didn't pan out, Judy would keep on getting better.

And making others better, too.

For now, she enjoyed the marvelous gift of being *home*.

With her loved ones.

ACKNOWLEDGMENTS

My first holiday collection saw the light of day in November 2021. Since then, I wrote several sweet romance short-stories, but never in the same genre. I have penned many short fiction pieces set in the holidays, even one time-travel Victorian tale, several mysteries, but no five who could jostle for space inside a themed collection. Until now.

I thanks the annual call for holiday stories by Kristine K. Rusch : I submitted several, but only got a few accepted, the time-travel story among those.

The book is dedicated to Jo Beverley, whom I had the joy to assist for some French dialogue in one historical romance.

Another warm and fuzzy feeling goes to my dad, Jacques E. Laframboise, and mother Thérèse Lorrain, dedicated readers. Both now reside among the stars.

And, finally, my big thanks go to you, reader and adventurer!

If you loved this collection, please make it known around you.

In our world intellectually threatened by a flood of AI-produced drivel, sharing your enthusiasm is the best thing you can do for human authors. May your words act as a beacon of light for the people craving new, hopeful stories!

ABOUT THE AUTHOR

Besides trying to initiate first contact with strange flora, Michèle Laframboise feeds coffee grounds to her garden plants, runs long distances and writes full time.

Fascinated by sciences and nature since she could walk, she has published 20 novels and more than 90 short-stories, earning a wide recognition in Canada and Europe. She is also a comic enthusiast who drew a dozen graphic novels and maintains an illustrated blog.

Her stories have been featured in *Asimov's, Analog, Fiction River, Compelling Science Fiction, Abyss&Apex, Solaris* and *Galaxies*. Holding degrees in geography and engineering, Michèle draws from her scientific background to create worlds filled with humor, invention and wonder.

Publisher's website: echofictions.com
Michèle's official website: michele-laframboise.com

facebook.com/michele.laframboise

instagram.com/michelesff

thecanadian.social/@Laframboise

linkedin.com/in/michele-laframboise

goodreads.com/Sundayartist

bsky.app/profile/savantefolle.bsky.social

ALSO BY MICHÈLE LAFRAMBOISE

5 Chocolate-Rich Holiday Stories

Holidays / upbeat romances / short-stories

When days get shorter, we crave the oldest of pick-me-ups, a good book and a cup of hot chocolate. Those five short-stories deal with trials and new beginnings, and how friendship or even love can bloom in the worst conditions, provided we never stop hoping for the best.

Five Holiday tales of compassion and courage, of wonders and sweetness penned by multi-award winner Michèle Laframboise.

5 Chocolate-Rich Holiday Stories, 132 pages

ISBN 978-1-988339-86-3 ebook

ISBN 978-1-988339-87-0 paperback

Michèle
LAFRAMBOISE
Multi-award winner author, Solaris and Aurora prizes recipient

White
Valentine

Sweet romance / meet cute / geek love

A fantasy geek locked out of his car in a raging snowstorm. A scarred-face woman at her window, her hopes waning as the snow piles on. Will they make this Valentine blind date?

A short heart-warming romance, told by multi-award winning author Michèle Laframboise

ISBN 978-1-988339-45-0 (ebook)

ISBN 978-1-988339-48-1 (print) 40 pages

More stories can be found at Echofictions.com

YEARNING FOR MORE STORIES?

Michèle Laframboise's full bibliography is enough to whet any SF reader's appetite!

Find out more books on Michèle's official site

New stories are brewing up constantly!

To get exclusive offers, some free readings, advanced information on special events,
join Michele's merry band of readers!
(Frequency: no more than one newsletter per month!)

FRIENDS' LIST

A story links every reader in a chain of friendship.
Feel free to write your name and give this book
to someone close.

❀

_____

_____

_____

_____

_____

_____

_____

_____